the GROWLY books

haven

the GROWLY books

haven

Philip & Erin Ulrich

Illustrated by Annie Barnett

Published by Here We Go Productions, LLC,
www.herewegoproductions.com.

ISBN-10: 0-9893852-4-8
ISBN-13: 978-0-9893852-4-4

Design and layout by Phil & Erin Ulrich, Design by Insight,
www.designbyinsight.net.

Illustrations by Annie Barnett, Be Small Studios,
www.besmallstudios.com.

Edited by Sandra Peoples, Next Step Editing,
www.nextstepediting.com.

Contents

to our two sweet adventurers . . .

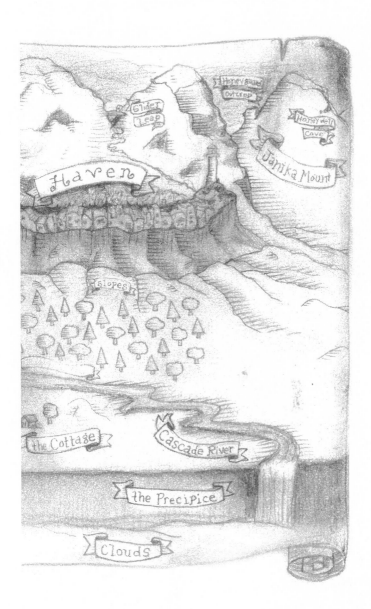

Honeydew
Outcrop

Glider
Leap

Honeydew
Cave

Haven

Janika Mount

slopes

the Cottage

Cascade River

the Precipice

Clouds

Ember

haven

1
The Great River

It thundered out of the mountains, miles to the north, up past the icy cliffs where no bear had ever been. *No bear except Hegel.* At least that's what the bears of Haven hoped. He had gone that way over a thousand years ago and was never seen again. "He must have made it past the Great River," the Elder Bears would say. "If anyone could find a way, Hegel could have."

The younger bears would nod excitedly. Of course *he* found a way. How could such a hero *not* find his long lost love: sweet Janika the Brave with the golden-yellow fur? But no bear since had found a way across. The river was over a mile wide, thundering and hissing with foam as it raced south toward The Precipice. Bears had ventured toward the Gulch, the gaping canyon where the Great River burst out of the mountains. One brave climber had even crept out onto the icy cliffs above the raging torrent. But no bear (since Hegel, of course!) had ever found a way across.

Ember sighed as she peered northward for a moment toward the misty haze that rose above the river. Even on the clearest days you could barely see the other side. The air was always swirling with icy spray, pushed northward by the howling winds that came up over the edge of The Precipice. What hope was there of seeing a tiny bird in all that haze? Even one that was brightly colored blue and red?

A loud rumble of thunder shook her from her thoughts, and she quickly turned back toward the south, where an enormous storm was racing in over the Lower Lands. Storms were common in Haven, but it was rare they looked like this. It was going to be a bad one.

"Oh, Growly," Ember whispered. There was no sign of him now. She had watched until his glider had gone out of sight around the back of Janika Mountain, a tiny speck in the shadow of the cliffs. Growly on Adventure! She could hardly believe the time had come. Ash was out there, and Skye and Gittel would leave in a few days. And then ... Ember felt her heart leap, "And then it will be me!"

Another clap of thunder echoed along the cliffs and seemed to shake the whole mountain. "Hurry up, Growly!" Ember breathed. A twinge of worry was there under all the excitement. He would be all right though. Growly was a sensible bear, *most* of the time. There was that occasion when he and Ash tried to put wheels on an old bathtub and ride it down through the apple meadow. And the time he almost fell in the Honey Well! Ember smiled to herself. He *was* a good bear ... most of the time. She missed him already. Ember was surprised at a sudden tear that trickled down her cheek.

"He'll be fine," she said after a moment, taking a deep breath. Her heart seemed like it was tossing and swirling, rushing this way and that like the waters of the Great River. She took another deep breath and turned back toward the north. That bird! Where could it have gone to? She had seen it. She was sure of that. Just for a moment, out of the corner of her eye. And then it had disappeared down into the Backland Valley. Where could it have gone?

Ember peered over the low wall that ran around the edge of Glider Leap. The valley was dark with shadows that crept up from the banks of the Cascade River far, far below. The cry of an eagle was faint somewhere in the distance, but there was no sign of the little bird. Ember followed the line of the Cascade River out toward the end of the valley, where it turned sharply and made its way down toward the Lower Lands and The Precipice. Beyond the curve of the Cascade River was another wide stretch of land called the Banks, and beyond that, the Great River. The bird couldn't have gone in that direction. Why would it?

Ember looked toward the Great River for a moment longer. She loved to stare out at the churning waters, especially from up here. At just the right moment you might catch a faint glimpse of green on the other side. You might see ... she suddenly gasped in surprise and almost stumbled backward. It ... it couldn't be! Ember's heart pounded as she blinked for a moment and then peered out at the Great River again. The air over there was thick with mist and haze, swirling in the dim light as the storm closed in. She had only seen it for a moment, but ...

Ember rubbed her eyes and, with her heart still pounding, glanced southward at the storm. It was coming quickly toward the mountains. There wasn't much time. With her legs feeling weak and trembly, she hurried across the platform to the stairs that led down into Glider Leap.

2
On Glider Leap

The stairs led down into the large storage room where the folded gliders were kept. There were empty spaces on some of the racks that lined the walls—Growly and Ash's storage places as well as those of other Cubs already out on Adventure. Ember glanced at her own glider for a moment as she rushed through the room. It was bundled and tied, leaning up against the wall with the long wing poles almost touching the high ceiling. She ran right by it and soon came to the far wall where a tall row of shelves stretched high above her. The shelves were stacked with ropes and climbing gear, as well as tools and ... there it was ... a long telescope.

Ember touched the cool, polished metal for a moment, trying to catch her breath and make sense of what she might have seen. A flash of light from across the Great River. Like fire in the thick woods that lined the banks of the far shore. Not like a forest fire though. It was like ... like a *signal* fire. She had just seen it for a moment before the cloud and spray hid it again from view. At least she *thought* she had seen it.

The telescope was long, almost as tall as Ember, and she swayed unsteadily as she took it down from the shelf and heaved it onto her shoulder. The smooth brass felt cool on her cheek as she stumbled across the room, moving as quickly as she could back toward the stairs. She was about to start her way upward when a loud clap of thunder boomed through the building, rattling the shelves and sending a metal plate clattering to the floor. Ember let out a shriek of surprise and then a moment later grinned. "Just thunder, Ember," she whispered to herself. "Just a little ... " Ember felt a sudden twinge of panic deep in her stomach, " ... just a little storm!" In all the excitement she had almost forgotten about the storm. She started up the stairs with a groan, straining to keep the telescope steady as she climbed.

Ember came out onto the roof again, puffing and panting as she made her way across the platform to a place on the western side of the parapet wall. There was a stand there, with a swiveling cradle. Ember hoisted the telescope up into place, fastening the clips that held it in the cradle. The wind whistled past her as she swung the lens around and put her eye up to the eyepiece. It took a moment to adjust the focus and find the right area on the far side of the river. Where was it? All she could see was spray and mist and the churning waters of the Great River. Another boom of thunder cracked above her, but Ember hardly noticed this time. Where was it? There was a brief flash of green as the mist cleared for a moment. Trees and grass and ... there! A sparkle of orange at the edge of the woods. Just for a moment, and then it was gone.

"No!" Ember cried as the mist closed back again and the spray and water were all she could see. She looked up from the telescope and peered in the direction of the river, hoping maybe the mist might clear again. She could feel the darkness of the storm closing in around her, and to the south she could see thick sheets of rain making their way steadily over the Lower Lands. Ember knew she had to get going. Unfastening the telescope, she heaved it on to her shoulder again and made her way back across the platform, her mind racing as she wondered about what she had seen. A forest fire? Perhaps. There was lightning in the air and it might have struck a tree. But something about it ...

Ember made her way down the stairs and across the storage room, lifting the telescope back up onto the shelf. There was something about that fire which had seemed ... had seemed like it was *made*. Ember shook her head. She had only seen the fire for a moment. There was no sense in imaging that it was *made*.

She came back outside again, hurrying out onto the rooftop as lightning flashed in the dark clouds to the south. "A forest fire," she whispered, nodding her head as if to say there could be no doubt. The other side of the Great River was lost in cloud and mist and gloom now, as the storm closed in on the mountains. Ember shivered a little as the cold wind whistled around her, ruffling her fur and flapping through her clothes.

"You'll want to wear long pants today," Merridy had told her that morning.

Ember had agreed. "But I'm wearing my best dress, too. It is a big day for ... for Growly that is." She had said that with a blush and wondered if Merridy noticed.

Merridy had looked at her quietly for a moment, a warm sparkle in her eyes. "Yes," she had said finally, giving Ember a wink, "long pants *and* a dress. That's just the thing for a day like this."

Now, Ember hurried down the steep, zig-zagging steps that cut across the cliffs just below Glider Leap. The steps were smooth and worn with age, but there were sturdy rails to hold onto, and if you didn't look down ... well, it wasn't *too* scary. Ember kept her eyes on her feet, and soon she reached the long platform leading from the cliffs to the gentler slopes on the side of the mountain. A narrow path cut along the ridge and then twisted its way on toward Haven.

When she reached the path, Ember took off at a run. She had traveled this way hundreds of times and knew every bump and turn all the way to the Lookout. The storm was almost here. Dark clouds and pounding rain were just ahead, howling up over the Lower Woods and almost to the Little Cliffs below Haven. Ember raced along the path, her boots crunching on the gravel and stones, her heartbeat pounding in her ears. The deafening howl of the wind surrounded her, growing stronger and stronger. Stinging splatters of rain were beginning to fall, and Ember wiped her eyes with her sleeve as she clambered down the slope. She could see the Lookout and the streets of Haven just beyond. A bear was running down the street, just a tiny speck from up this high, holding his hat as he ran.

Ember pushed on, gasping for breath as she made her way downward. Raindrops were all around now. Little splatters in the dust at first, joining with other splatters until the path was slick and wet. Ember's dress was soon soaked and clung about her as she ran, slipping and sliding on the muddy stones. The wind screamed in her ears, and as she looked down toward Haven, she could see twisting swirls of rain washing over the rooftops. The flags and banners on the town hall whipped wildly in the wind, and as she watched, one of them flew off and away, swirling up into the mountains.

The wind was so strong now that Ember had to push against it, and the stinging rain made it almost impossible to see. She wiped the water out of her eyes again and peered through the dimness. Just a little further to the Lookout. Just a few more turns and ...

Whoosh! Ember felt her boots slip on the muddy path, and she was tumbling and sliding down the slick, grassy slope. She finally came to a stop with a jolting, sloshing thud in a large puddle at the bottom. Pounding rain and wind whipped along the path in twists and swirls. Ember clambered to her feet and leaned against the torrent as she made her way slowly toward a dim shape just ahead. The Lookout. It was not far now. It was not home, but at least it would be shelter. Ember could feel her muscles aching. The race down the mountain had not been easy. And the tumble down the slope—ouch! The stone walls of the Lookout rose up into the darkness, disappearing into the rain and storm. Just a little further. Ember pushed against the wind, her fur matted and muddy and her face aching from the pelting rain.

"Ember!" The sound of a shout cut through the howling around her. A dark figure had just come out of the Lookout and was running toward her down the muddy path.

3
The Lookout

"Mama!" Ember gasped as she sloshed through a deep puddle and into Merridy's outstretched arms.

The older bear held her close for a moment before motioning toward the Lookout. "Come on!" she shouted, doing her best to be heard above the howling wind as she hurried Ember toward the open doorway.

There were two other bears standing just inside, and as Ember came closer she recognized Growly's grandparents, Fergal and Mika. They both looked a little worried, but when Ember and Merridy came into the warmth and the door was shut tight against the storm, Fergal's face lit in a wide grin and Mika let out a chuckle.

"Look at you two!" Mika said at last, shaking her head. "Merridy! You look like you've just been for a swim and ... Ember? Is that you under all that mud?"

Ember grinned, but Mika didn't wait for an answer. "Stay right here," she said, and then turned and hurried off through a door on the far side of the room.

They were standing in the main meeting room of the Lookout. It was a wide, bright place, with lamps around the walls and a blazing fireplace to the left. There was a bedroom off to the right, and that is where Mika had just gone.

"There's towels in here," she called, "and you can wrap in blankets until you warm up."

Fergal gave Ember a wink. "She might send Merridy to bed without any supper," he said in a mischievous whisper.

Ember giggled.

"I heard that, Fergal *my dear*!" Mika said as she came through the doorway. She was doing her best to look serious, but her eyes sparkled and there was a hint of a grin at the corners of her mouth. Mika hurried over and wrapped fresh, dry towels around Merridy and Ember.

"What a storm!" Mika said after a moment, looking up at the pounding rain on the window and shaking her head in wonder. "We were about to come looking for you when Merridy spotted you on the path."

"I don't think I've seen one like this," Merridy agreed. "Did you see how fast it came up from The Precipice? It was here in less than an hour."

Ember was rubbing her head with the towel, and she looked down at the muddy puddle around her. "I would have been back sooner," she said, still trying to catch her breath, "but I saw something, and ..."

"The bird?!" Merridy gasped. Her face was full of hope.

"Oh yes!" Ember cried. She had almost forgotten seeing the little blue and red bird. "Mama! I saw him! Just for a moment, but I saw him, *too*!"

Merridy's eyes filled with tears, and she turned to Fergal and Mika with a weak smile. "He *is* here!" she whispered.

Mika put her arm around Merridy and gave her a tight hug. "He's probably waiting out the storm in one of the mountain caves, Merridy. Oh ... this is *great* news."

Merridy smiled at her friend and wiped the tears away with her towel.

"He flew down below Glider Leap. On the Backland Valley side," Ember said excitedly. "It was just before Growly left, and I didn't see him again, but ... " Ember felt a little a little embarrassed. " ... but I saw something *else* too, I think."

Merridy, who had been drying the fur around her ears, paused and looked seriously at Ember. Fergal leaned closer, his eyes bright and alert. "What did you see?" he asked kindly.

"A fire!" Ember said. "A fire on the other side of the Great River!"

Fergal blinked in surprise. "You could see the other side?"

Ember nodded. "Just for a moment. But I ran and got the big telescope, and I saw it again."

"A forest fire from the lightning. It must be," Mika said. She looked at Fergal, and the way she spoke sounded almost like a question.

"At first I thought it *must* be," Ember said earnestly, "but the storm hadn't reached that side yet, and there was just something about it." She looked down at the floor, feeling a little silly.

"Yes. You would know a forest fire if you saw one," Mika said with a nod and an encouraging smile. Ember looked up and smiled back gratefully.

"Well," Merridy said, putting her arm around Ember's shoulder. "There'll be no fire out in that storm ... and there won't be much chance of spotting a little blue and red bird either." Merridy sounded concerned as she continued, "Oh, I hope Growly and Ash found shelter before the rain arrived."

Ember smiled. "He was past Janika Mountain long before the storm hit. He may not have had time to fill up his jar at the Honey Well though," she added with a giggle. "And Ash left a long time before him."

"I'm sure he's sitting in a cave having the time of his life right now, honey or no honey," Fergal said. "What a way for a Cub to start his Adventure. Now, why don't we go to the top of the Lookout and watch the storm?" There was a sparkle of adventure in the older bear's eyes, and Mika poked him with her elbow.

"Alright," she said, trying to look serious again. "But don't go leaning way out of the window the way you like to do. You know that makes my stomach queasy!"

"And I don't want to go chasing after your hat!" Merridy added with a laugh as they made their way toward the twisting staircase on the far side of the room.

It was a long climb to the top. The stairway spiraled up past storerooms and landings, higher and higher, till at last they came out into a large, round room with windows all the way around. The windows were closed tight with strong wooden storm shutters that rattled and creaked in the gale.

"Whoa! Can you feel the floor swaying?" Fergal asked with a mischievous grin.

"Fergal!" Mika scolded with a frown that had the hint of a smile mixed in. "If this tower is swaying it's because *you* ate too much lunch. Now, let's have a look at this storm."

There were four large telescopes: one looking out toward The Precipice, one toward the Great River, one toward Glider Leap, and the other pointing eastward along the Lower Lands and the cliffs where the mountains started. The telescopes were mounted in round holes in the wall that were sealed with strong, waterproof material. On a clear day you could see for miles in all directions. Ash had once spotted an eagle above the trees on the other side of the Great River. And the Mayor had once seen a glider as far away as the Apple Valley, which was many, many miles to the east. In this storm though, there was nothing to see but twisting sheets of rain and bright flashes of lightning cutting through the gloom. It was still daytime, but with the storm raging all around, it was almost as dark as night.

"I can't see a thing!" Ember called, stepping back from her telescope.

Merridy was peering through the telescope that pointed towards The Precipice. "I think I can see some rain!" she laughed.

Fergal gazed longingly at the two rattling, wooden doors leading to the outside walkway. "I think we might see more out there," he called, that familiar spark of adventure in his eyes.

"Well," Mika grinned, "just leave your hat inside, my dear."

"Ready?" Fergal called, grabbing hold of the door handles with both paws.

"Just a quick look," Mika said urgently. "But don't go to the edge of the walkway. With this lightning ..."

Fergal pulled the doors open with an excited shout and had to steady himself in the sudden rush of wind and rain. "What a storm!" he cried as his hat flew off his head and twisted across the room.

"Look at that rain!" Mika laughed, pushing her way toward her husband. Her eyes were sparkling. The truth is, she loved storms, too.

The sound of wind and thunder roared around the room, and Merridy had to shout to make herself heard above the din. "It's a big one, that's for sure. Better close those doors soon, or we'll need a boat in here."

"Oh, Growly," Ember whispered, as Fergal and Mika pushed the big doors closed again. "I hope you found a dry place ... wherever you are."

4
The Storm

"**M**erridy! Merridy!" Ember heard the faint shout coming from below. It was Gittel's voice. Ember recognized it right away, even through the roar of the storm. Skye would probably be with her. She almost always was. Skye, Gittel, and Ember had been close friends for as long as any of them could remember.

"We're up here!" Ember called, shouting as loud as she could down the stairwell. "Wait there! We're coming down!"

Fergal, Mika, and Merridy were almost done mopping up the puddles of rain with towels, and soon they all hurried down the stairs toward the meeting room at the base of the tower. Gittel and Skye stood near the main door, their coats slick and soaking and dripping into puddles around their boots. Gittel had her apron on under her raincoat, and if she hadn't been so wet, there would have been streaks of flour in her fur from the bakery. Gittel's father was the finest baker in Haven, and her mother's apple cakes were legendary. Gittel's kitchen skills were already the talk of the village.

Skye had her flying cap on, of course, with her goggles perched up on her forehead and a wide grin of adventure spread across her face. Skye had the right name, that's for sure. Ember smiled at the thought. If Skye wasn't up in her glider, she was almost always talking about it. And she *always* wore her cap.

"Ember!" Gittel panted as the four bears came into the meeting room. "Have you been out in it, too?"

Ember nodded and ran over to give her dripping friends a hug. "I was up on Glider Leap." Ember suddenly grinned as she realized she was still wrapped in a blanket. "I slid down half the mountain, I think! And landed in a mud puddle!"

Skye giggled, but her face quickly went serious again, and she turned to the three older bears. "One of the storm shutters has blown off at the library. Gittel's father doesn't think the window will hold for long. A window at the bakery is already broken! Daddy went to check next door at the library once he got it boarded up. He thinks we can save the window at the library if we can board it up, too. But it will need all of us in this wind. It feels like the whole of Haven is rattling and creaking!"

"We'll get it boarded," Ember said, trying to sound as encouraging as she could. Still, she felt a shiver run down her back.

"Let's go," Merridy said with a worried smile. "It won't be just the library that needs help. I think we're in for a long night!"

•••••••••••••••••••••

The streets of Haven were filled with the howl and clamor of the storm. Signs swung wildly above the doorways of offices and stores. Shutters creaked and groaned as the wind and rain whipped and whistled along the cliff face. Bears shouted as they ran here and there, hammering boards over windows and chasing whatever the storm tossed about. Thunder boomed overhead and echoed along the cliffs. Above it all was the constant howl of the wind and the clatter of rain on the rooftops.

"There it is!" shouted Merridy to the others, as they pushed against the downpour, making their way slowly down the main street. "I can hardly recognize a thing, but there's the library!"

There was a sudden burst of wind as Merridy opened the library door. She almost lost her balance as the small group stumbled and bustled into the entryway, soaked and dripping. Fergal and the girl Cubs heaved the heavy wooden door shut again, straining with all their might until the latch fell in place and a sudden stillness filled the hall. Merridy was already making her way toward the main room, flinging her coat to the side and kicking off her shoes as she hurried.

"There are towels in the hall closet," she called, disappearing through a side doorway. And then her voice could be heard from the main library room. "Farren! You're here, too! And thank you, Adwin! The window is still holding."

Ember stumbled into the library with the rest of the group close behind. As her eyes grew used to the bright lamplight, Ember could see Growly's father, Farren, busily tying a thick piece of rope around his waist, while Gittel's father, Adwin, tied the other end around one of the thick wooden pillars near the door.

"You're not going out in this!" Ember gasped, as Farren finished tying the rope and gave it a tug to make sure it was secure.

Farren grinned and gave her a wink. "It's a big one, isn't it?" he said. "I just wish I had a bar of soap. I could have a shower while I'm out there."

Adwin was tying a length of rope around his stomach now, and he looked over at Farren with a smile.

"You're going too, Daddy?" Gittel asked with a hint of worry in her voice. She was proud of him though, and she threw her arms around Adwin and pressed her cheek against his shoulder.

"It won't be long," he said as he gave her a little squeeze. "That is, unless Farren decides to sing some

Adventure songs while he takes his shower! I just plan to re-close the shutters and nail up these boards and then be home in time to bake a loaf or two before bedtime."

With that, he made his way over to a small door leading out onto the ledge that ran along the cliff side of the library. Farren followed close behind. Soon the two of them were inching their way along the ledge toward the flailing shutter, which had come off of one of its hinges. Fergal stood at the open doorway, ready to pass out long lengths of board that would be nailed up once the shutter was back in place. Merridy and Mika held up towels, trying to stop as much rain from coming in as they could. The floor was soon soaked though. Ember, Skye, and Gittel raced about, moving books to the far side of the room and mopping up the puddles as best as they could.

The two bears outside inched their way along the ledge, staying close to the building and trying not to look down. The storm made it hard to see far, but when lightning flashed you could see all the way down to the bottom of the cliffs—a long, *long* way down.

Farren reached the broken shutter, and getting down on his knees, he crawled under and then pushed against the heavy wood with all his might. The shutter was twice as tall as he was, and with the force of the wind it was all he could do to even get it to budge.

"Pull it around!" he shouted to Adwin. The baker nodded and pulled the shutter until it finally began to swing. "It's going to come around fast!" Farren cried as the wind suddenly caught the shutter and twisted it toward the window. The warning was almost too late, and Adwin had to scramble backward as the heavy wood whooshed by and slammed against the building with a jarring thud.

"See if you can hold it in place!" Farren shouted as the baker scrambled to his feet. "The second hinge looks like it's about to break. If it does the whole thing will fly off into the storm!"

Adwin pushed against the shutter as Farren took a hammer from his work belt and began to pound long iron nails through the wood and into the window frame. "Now the boards!" he cried, and Adwin turned and began to pull the planks through the doorway and out onto the ledge.

Everyone inside had been anxiously watching the two bears work, hardly daring to breathe. When the shutter had slammed shut, Gittel had let out a cry and Merridy had gasped.

"They're OK!" Fergal assured them after sticking his head out the door and peering down the ledge through the rain.

It was impossible to see anything from inside now. The minutes dragged by, feeling like hours to the anxious bears inside the library. The sound of hammering was reassuring, and Fergal stuck his head through the doorway from time to time to check that the two bears were still out there. They all breathed a sigh of relief when Adwin's face finally appeared in the doorway, closely followed by Farren's. Both of them were soaked and dripping, and both wore wild, adventurous grins.

5
Legends

Ember stared down at the hot mug of tea in her paws, watching the twisting wisps of steam as they twirled up into the dimness. It was evening now, and she and Merridy sat alone on the over-stuffed couch that faced the big, shuttered windows in the library. The storm still roared outside, but there was a peaceful stillness that hung in the room, a hush that even the rattling windows and the booming thunder couldn't shake.

This was her favorite place. Sitting right here on the couch with Merridy, sipping tea and talking in the quiet hours before bed. Usually the shutters were open, and on clear nights the sky was bright and bristling with stars. When the moon was full, the Lower Lands were bathed in a silvery glow, so bright that even at midnight you could see all the way to The Precipice.

"Do you remember the storm when you were little? The one when my bedroom window broke?" Merridy's voice startled Ember from her thoughts, making her jump and almost spill her tea. They had been sitting silently for a long time, looking out into the dimness and listening to the storm.

"I think so," Ember said, looking up with a smile. "I think I remember we sat right here. I remember sitting on your lap and snuggling because I was scared, and then feeling happy. The storm sounded nice once I felt safe with you."

Merridy nodded and smiled at the memory. "You were so little. You'd only been with me less than a year. We sat here for hours and then made beds with pillows on the library floor. I sang you songs and told you stories until we both fell asleep and awoke to birds and sunshine and fresh mountain air."

"And a mountain of pancakes!" Ember added with a grin.

"Yes! Everyone came by for breakfast!" Merridy said with a laugh. "At least it seemed like everyone!"

They sat quietly for a moment, remembering the library full of all the friends and family who had come to check on them after the storm.

"I don't remember much before then," Ember said, looking back at Merridy thoughtfully. "There's little scenes and flashes of feelings ... Haven seemed bigger, of course!" Ember grinned. "I think I remember Growly. Before that ... " Ember reached as far back in her memory as she could, " ... I remember splashes of water, and ... " Ember leaned closer to Merridy, reaching her paw tenderly toward the older bear's face. "I remember your cheek—the color of the fur and the little streaks of white. Isn't it funny that's one of the first things I remember?"

Merridy had tears in her eyes. "Oh Ember, you were so little! You threw your tiny arms around my neck and wouldn't let go. I carried you all the way to Haven with your cheek pressed up against mine."

Merridy took a deep breath and wiped a runaway tear with the back of her paw. "And look at you now! So beautiful and grown up. Growly's out on Adventure and yours will start in a few days."

Ember put her mug on the floor and wrapped her arms around the older bear, pressing her cheek against Merridy's. "Thank you," she whispered. "Thank you for choosing me."

Merridy leaned back and smiled at Ember through tears that were flowing freely now. "I had been down in the Lower Lands, in the hills near the Banks. I was out exploring when I saw someone in the distance, down toward the Great River. It was Macon, the mayor's brother, and as I got closer I could see he had a bundle in his arms. When I first saw you, wrapped in a blanket and shivering, my heart almost broke. And when everyone saw how you clung to me, how you wouldn't let me go for a moment, well ... we all knew you should come to live with me at the library."

An extra loud crack of thunder suddenly shook the room, making the lamps rattle as it echoed along the cliffs. Ember usually loved storms, but this one seemed to be growing by the hour. Growly would be fine. She had stopped worrying about him a while back. He would be having the time of his life, bundled up in one of the mountain caves with a roaring fire, singing silly Adventure songs as he watched the lightning. He'd probably even cheer as the thunder got louder. Growly would have some stories to tell at the end of the summer. "We'll both be Young Bears then," she thought to herself with a smile, though right now she was feeling a lot like a Cub.

"Shall we read a story while we wait for the storm to pass?" Merridy asked.

Ember smiled and nodded. "*Twelve Foot Hegel and His Flying Wheelbarrow?*"

Merridy let out a happy laugh. "Yes! That would be just the thing!" It was their special joke. The book was really called *Hegel the Mighty*, one of the many books on the founder of Haven. So many books had been written about Hegel that there was a whole aisle dedicated to him. Picture books, histories, novels, and even a series of cookbooks! And then there was *Hegel the Mighty*. A "history" book written six hundred years ago that seemed, well, a *little* farfetched.

"*He was far taller than any bear, perhaps twelve feet tall, and once pulled down a mountain pine tree with his 'bare' paws and carried it eighteen miles through the mountains.*" That was just in the first chapter, and the stories got even wilder (and of course, funnier) as the book went on.

Ember took the book from the shelf and carried it back over to the couch. "What do you think he was really like, Mama?" she asked as she sat back down beside Merridy. She had asked that question many times, as every Cub did. Hegel and his love, Janika, were heroes, and every Cub wanted to be like them. The problem was there were so many stories, and each one seemed different than the other.

Merridy smiled. "Don't tell anyone," she whispered with a wink, "but I think he was a little shorter than twelve feet. Probably just eleven and three quarters!"

Ember giggled.

"No," Merridy continued, her face looking thoughtful, "I think he was probably not much different than us. He was a hero, that is for certain, but I think more than anything he was just a bear like us who made good choices at a time when those choices were very hard to make. It was the times they were in that made the choices seem big. And it's time gone by that has turned him into a legend."

Merridy got up off the couch and made her way over to the shelves of books, searching down the rows until she found the one she was looking for. "Here it is," she said, returning to the couch. She brushed through the pages and nodded as she found the right one.

"*Time turns a turnip into honeycake,*" Merridy read, smiling as she added, "and everyday heroes into legends. Now. Shall we read about about *twelve foot Hegel?*"

Ember nodded, and Merridy was just turning to the first page when there was a sudden pounding on the front door and shouts of alarm from the street.

6
Into the Night

Farren stood in the doorway. Growly's father was bundled up in his heavy coat with the hood almost hiding his face. Rain pelted him, splattering against his side and whipping in a twisting spray back off again into the gale.

"Come in!" Merridy gasped. There were other bears in the street, too. Ember could see their shapes in the darkness, running from door to door and shouting to be heard above the noise of the storm.

"There's no time!" Farren cried, shaking his head. "We need you both at the Town Hall now! Dress for the storm and bring your emergency kits!"

Merridy gasped, and was about to ask a question when Farren took off into the rain.

Heaving the big door closed again, Merridy turned to Ember with determination in her eyes. "You get the kits, Ember! I'll get our boots and coats ready! Now hurry!"

She hardly needed to say it. Ember was already running down the hall. She knew exactly where the emergency kits were. Two backpacks were kept in a cupboard at the entrance to the library room. Kneeling by the packs, she quickly checked the straps to make sure everything was fastened tight.

"Get two of the outdoor lamps," Merridy's voice called from somewhere upstairs, "and extra oil." There was a thumping sound on the stairs, and Merridy appeared around the corner, coats and heavy hiking pants bundled in her arms. They got dressed right there in the hallway, fastening their jackets tight and double knotting the laces on their boots. Merridy did a final check on Ember's pack and nodded. "Here we go," she said, taking a deep breath, and with the rain and wind whipping around them, they pushed out into the night.

The Town Hall entry room was packed with bears, all of them bundled in heavy coats and thick hiking pants, and every one of them soaked and dripping. It was the Rescue Committee. They were all trained in climbing and exploration and in search and rescue and simple medicine. Farren was the leader of the group—he had been since Growly was a baby Cub. It was not Farren who addressed the group first though. The mayor stepped onto a small podium, looking worried and tired.

"Thank you for coming so quickly," he said with a nod to the gathered group. He spoke simply and seriously. "We would not have called you out in this storm if it were not an emergency. Wynton and Merritt are missing! They were down in the Lower Lands this morning. Probably out toward the Banks."

Ember gasped. Wynton was one of the Elder Bears. He was a builder and had built Ember's glider. And Merritt was his young granddaughter.

Farren stepped up beside the mayor. "Wynton would have known to return at the first sign of the storm in the distance," he said gravely. "Even in this rain he could find his way back. We must assume he is injured. I know it is dangerous to go out in a storm like this, but the mayor and I both agree we have to try and find the two of them right away. This storm could last a long time." His voice went a little quieter, and Ember could see the deep worry in his eyes. "I am asking for thirty volunteers to come with me."

He had hardly finished the sentence when every bear in the room raised a paw. Some of them raised two!

Farren smiled thankfully. "Just as I thought you would!" he said in admiration. He pulled a list from his pocket. "Many of you will be needed here, though I felt sure you would all want to go. I have made a list of those who know the Lower Lands best. Those not on the list will stay here with the mayor to deal with the needs in Haven. Those on the list, follow me into the meeting room."

Farren began to read out the names. Merridy, Fergal, and Mika were on there, of course. No one knew the Lower

Lands better than they did. Ember was not surprised to hear Skye's name either. And when Ember's name was read out, many of the bears nodded in agreement and patted her on the back. The Lower Lands were like her second home.

As their names were read, the search team filed through the tall double doors into the meeting room of the Town Hall. Lamps lined the walls, and the long tables were piled with ropes and blankets and bundles of dried fruit and nuts.

"Take a length of rope and a blanket and as much food as you can fit in your pack," Farren instructed. "Tie one end of your rope around your waist, and the other end to the bear next to you. We will travel in groups of three. The ropes will keep you from losing each other in the storm. As soon as you are ready, come over to the side door. We're heading for the Westwind Caverns. That will be our home base for the search."

Before long, the bears were making their way down the main street and then out toward the path that cut down the face of the Little Cliffs. The wind howled up from the Lower Lands, driving pelting, stinging rain up the side of Mount Hegel. It was slow going and dangerous. The pathway was fairly wide, but the force of the storm made the little groups stumble and sway as they journeyed downward. The Little Cliffs were only little when you compared them to The Precipice, and it was all the bears could do to stay steady on the path and not be blown off into the Lower Lands far below.

Ember tugged at the rope around her waist, checking it again to make sure it was good and tight. She was tied between Skye, who was leading the way, and Merridy, who would (hopefully) be the anchor if one of them slipped. The wind pushed against them from all directions, and the rocky path down the cliff face was a muddy river that made the journey very slow and very dangerous.

"Can you see the bottom yet?" Ember shouted to Skye. Skye was just a dim shape up ahead, but the light of her lamp cut through the stormy night. Ember saw her nod.

"One more turn!" Skye's voice seemed muffled and distant because of the coat hood that covered Ember's ears.

Next would come the foothills, and about half a mile further would be the Westwind Caverns. Up ahead, Ember thought she could see the bobbing glow of the lamps of some of the others. There were two more groups behind them. She caught a glimpse of them from time to time.

As they came to the foothills, the little group left the path, taking off at a faster pace over the grassy slopes and doing their best not to slide in the rain. Skye tugged twice on the rope, and Ember did the same. This signaled to Merridy that they should head up toward the tall boulders at the base of the cliffs. It would not be good to stay out on the open slopes with all the lightning in the air.

Reaching the boulders, they twisted their way along the base of the cliff, keeping their heads low as they wove between the rocks. It was slow going, but at least it wasn't as windy as it had been coming down the path. The enormous rocks shielded them from some of the rain, too. Ember was glad of that.

"There it is!" Skye shouted as she came around a large boulder and saw a wide stretch of open cliffs just up ahead. A gaping cavern rose high above them, firelight flickering on the walls from somewhere within. Ember watched as the group ahead turned and then disappeared inside. They had come to the mouth of the Westwind Caverns.

7
The Search

As they came into the wide opening, Ember breathed a sigh of relief. The noise of the wind and pelting rain fell behind them. She pulled back the hood of her coat and grinned as Skye did the same. Even under her hood, Skye was wearing her flight cap.

Ember could make out the sound of voices now, and as they came around a bend she saw the dripping huddle of bears that made up the rest of the group. They were standing in a large room, sheltered from the wind, with a blazing fire in the large hearth on the far wall. There were long tables by the wall near the fireplace and chairs scattered throughout the room. Lamps bathed the area in a warm glow. This was not the biggest space in the Westwind Caverns, but it was the most used. The tables and chairs were always here, and there were beds in other rooms nearby. No one lived here, but the place was used for storing food gathered in the Lower Lands. Most bears spent a few nights a month down here, when it was their time to search for food.

"Keep your ropes on!" Farren's voice came from the side of the room near the tables. He had his hood pulled back, but he was still carrying his pack and rope tied around his waist. "We'll go out right away. Just leave your blankets and most of your food. There are ten teams. We will all go out for the rest of the night. Maps are laid out on the tables with the search routes marked for each team. You must stay on the route you are given."

Farren sighed. Ember could see he was tired and worried. When he spoke again, his voice was quieter. "We can only cover a small area. And with all this rain, we could walk right by them and never know it. But we might find them, too. They may see the light of our lamps. Regardless ... *we have to try*."

There were determined nods all around the room. Everyone knew how difficult the search would be.

"We meet back here at dawn," Farren continued. "If we haven't found them by then, we will start going out in shifts. We will all need to rest. Now, line up in your groups near the tables to get your map and directions. And be careful out there."

It wasn't long till they were standing again at the mouth of the caverns, looking out into the rain as it thundered down. Ember watched the group ahead disappear into the night, their lamplight swallowed up by the darkness of the storm.

"Ready?" Merridy asked with a shaky smile. She put her arms around the two younger bears and squeezed them tightly. "I'm proud of you both," she whispered. "Don't lose your cap," she said, giving Skye a wink.

Skye grinned and pulled the hood of her coat up over her head (and cap).

Turning to Ember, Merridy said, "Keep us on the path, dear. You know this area the best."

Ember nodded. "OK," she said, taking a deep breath. "To the apple grove." As they left the shelter of the cave, she felt the sudden slap of wind and rain against her face again. Ember tried to pull her hood tighter, but it didn't help much. She looked to her left along the line of rope to where the dim glow of Skye's lamp could be seen bobbing through the rain. And there was Merridy's lamp, just off to her right.

They made their way along the face of the cliffs for a while and then cut off down the slopes toward the west. It was slow going. Ember had to stop and check for landmarks every few minutes, shielding her eyes with her paw and trying to make out familiar places in the darkness and rain.

"Take it slowly," Merridy encouraged, coming over as Ember stood and peered ahead into the storm.

"I can hardly see a thing, Mama!" Ember whimpered, looking up at the older bear. "I don't want to get us lost!"

"You won't," Merridy said.

There was a sureness in Merridy's voice that seemed to soak into Ember and calm her growing panic. She nodded, and gave Merridy a shaky smile.

Lightning flashed suddenly.

"I think that's Morrigan's Marbles just ahead," she gasped, pointing to a jumbled pile of boulders in the distance.

They pushed on into the night, moving slowly westward as they searched for the two lost bears. There was no point in calling out. The noise of the storm was too loud. But they waved their lanterns as they went, looking behind every tree and boulder on their path.

It was well after midnight when they finally came through a thick stretch of woods and out onto the rise that sloped down toward the apple grove. Just beyond the grove would be the Cascade River, and beyond the Cascade you would come to the Banks. They wouldn't be searching that far though. Ember crouched down and pulled out the folded map from her coat pocket. Skye and Merridy huddled around her, trying to make a little shelter from the rain and holding their lanterns so Ember could read the map.

"We're to search the grove," Ember shouted. "That's the most likely place in this area they would have gone. We'll also search along the banks of the Cascade, from here to here," she added, pointing to a shaded area on the map.

"We'll need to stay close through the apple trees," Merridy shouted, holding up her rope, "so we don't get tangled."

"Let's go," Ember shouted. "Skye, you lead the way."

Skye nodded, and with a grin she pulled her flight goggles down from her forehead. "At least my eyes will be dry!" she yelled and patted Ember softly on the back.

With Skye leading, the little group set off again, making their way quickly down the grassy slope and into the trees.

There was some shelter from the storm under the thick, leafy branches of the apple trees. Skye led them on a twisting search, going from tree to tree until finally they came to the far side of the grove. "If they came here, they're not here now," she shouted. Her voice was always a little croaky, but Ember could see her friend was about to cry, and her voice sounded ragged and hoarse. Wynton and his family were good friends of Skye's, and everyone loved little Merritt.

"We'll find them, Skye," Ember said, giving her friend a comforting hug. "Someone will," she added. "Let's search along the Cascade. We'll need to start heading back soon if we're to reach the cave by morning."

They made their way out of the grove and up a hill toward a distant, low, rumbling sound. As they came to the top of the hill they were met with the roaring thunder of the Cascade River. The sound of it rose even above the noise of the storm. A flash of lightning lit the area all around them, and Ember gasped. "Look at the size of it!" she cried. "I have never seen it this full!"

The Cascade River was never small, and in this part of the Lower Lands it always rushed and rumbled as it raced south toward The Precipice. But now it was a churning, pounding torrent, stretching out toward the west farther than the eye could see.

"How did it get so big this quickly," Merridy gasped, "even with all this rain?"

"Come on!" Skye cried. "If they're down by the river, they could *really* be in danger!"

With Skye still leading, they hurried down the slope toward the river, making their way southward. The grass was slick and slippery with mud. Ember looked down nervously at the churning river. Logs and branches hurtled by in the darkness, tossed and toppled in the rapids.

"Ember!" Skye cried, as the grass suddenly gave way under her feet. Skye was sliding in a muddy avalanche, headed straight toward the water.

Ember turned to Merridy in panic, but the older bear was already bounding up the slope, shouting to Ember as she went. "Get up the slope!" she cried. "Get as high as you can and dig in!"

Ember leaped into action, scrambling up the slope as quickly as she could.

"Ember! Merridy!"

Ember felt a jolting tug on her rope that almost knocked her off her feet.

"Dig in!" Merridy cried.

Ember dropped to the ground and slammed her heels into the soft, muddy grass. The rope was tight and shaking, and Ember felt herself starting to slip. "Mama!"

Suddenly Merridy was at her side, the older bear's face straining as she began to heave on Ember's rope. Nothing seemed to happen at first, and then, slowly, the rope began to move. There was a shout in the darkness, and suddenly Skye's frightened face appeared through the rain, as she scrambled up the riverbank and fell panting and gasping into Merridy's arms.

8
Gittel's Pancakes

Ember sat wrapped in a blanket, watching the flickering flames dance in the fireplace. They had made it back to the caverns half an hour ago, tired and soaked and discouraged by not finding the missing bears. Six of the groups were already there when they arrived. As she sat warming up, Ember could hear the shouts of another group coming in out of the storm.

Next to Ember, Skye sat with her head resting tiredly in her hands. Skye's flight cap was lying on the floor beside her, and the bear's dark, chocolate brown fur looked damp and matted. Ember reached over and gave Skye's head a friendly rub. It was rare to see her without her cap.

"Maybe one of the last groups has found them," Ember said, trying to sound encouraging. "And if not, we'll be heading out again as soon as Farren returns."

Skye nodded tiredly and tried to smile, but Ember could see she was close to tears. They had continued searching along the riverbank for an hour and then searched all the way back to the caverns. Ember felt on the verge of tears, too. They were all worried and exhausted.

Ember looked up at the sound of Merridy's voice. She was over by the tables with Fergal and Mika. Maps were stretched out in front of them, and they were talking earnestly as they discussed the terrain and where the search should focus next. "There are caves down past the bridge," she was saying. "They could have gone there for shelter." She didn't sound sure about it though. The truth was they could be *anywhere*. And in this weather ...

Farren's voice suddenly boomed from the cavern entrance. "Have they been found?" he asked someone. Then he called out, "Gather up! We're going out again." He came around the corner, soaking and dripping with his hood still over his head. Farren looked quickly around the room at the exhausted bears and asked quietly, "Which teams will volunteer for the first shift?"

Skye was already on her feet, and she raised her paw high. "I'm ready!" she said with a sniffle. Bears all around the room were beginning to stand. Some of them wobbled with exhaustion, but all of them were ready to go back out.

"We'll have five teams," Farren said, counting them off as he looked around the room. "My parents have been planning the next search areas. All teams on the first shift line up at the tables for your instructions. Everyone else, please get some rest. We may have a long day ahead of us."

Dawn was breaking as they went out again. There was no sunrise to be seen and no break in the rain—just a slight brightening in the blackness to show that the sun was shining somewhere up above the storm.

Ember, Skye, and Merridy searched for hours along their route, stumbling through the downpour until midday. They slept through the afternoon while the second shift searched, and when evening came, they prepared to go out again.

"Ember," Farren's voice greeted her from across the busy meeting room as she entered. "Skye."

The two Cubs looked over to where Growly's father was standing with three other Young Bears. "We need you five to be ready," he stated, as Skye and Ember joined the little group. "I don't know when this storm will end, but as soon as it does, as soon as there is daylight, we will need to search from the air."

Skye's face brightened at the mention of flying, and Ember nodded seriously. They could cover much more ground from the air.

"Merridy has been helping me map out search areas for you. If you see Wynton and Merritt, land as quickly as possible and start a signal fire. We'll have bears watching from the Lookout, and from the Lower Land towers, too."

Skye squeezed Ember's paw excitedly, and the other Young Bears nodded.

"Now tie yourselves together and head back to Haven. Get a good sleep, as you need to be ready to fly early if the storm breaks tonight."

The journey back to Haven took a long time. The little group slipped and stumbled on the rocky path, making their way slowly and carefully as they twisted their way up the side of the Little Cliffs.

When they arrived in Haven, the village looked dark and abandoned, with all the windows shuttered up and the streets empty. The Cubs untied their ropes and went off to their homes to rest, Ember giving Skye a hug as the rain pelted down on them and the wind whipped past their ears.

Ember would be staying with Gittel tonight. The bakery was right next to the library. There was even an inside doorway joining the two buildings. Ember always stayed at Gittel's when Merridy was out.

Ember pounded on the bakery door and after a moment heard Gittel's happy shout from inside. "It's Ember!! Pour some tea!"

The door swung wide, and Ember was pulled inside as Gittel wrapped her in a tight hug and then began to help her with her coat and pack. "You're soaking!" Gittel said, and the next moment was calling, "Mama! Blankets! We need blankets! And tea and ..."

Ember smiled. Gittel always knew how to look after you.

Soon Ember was sitting on the long couch in the living room, sipping hot tea and telling Gittel and her family about the search. It was good to be in dry clothes again. Gittel had already laid them out for her on the spare bed, along with her toothbrush and pillow. She had brought them from the library as soon as she heard Ember was coming.

When Ember finished telling about the search, Gittel's father shook his head in amazement. "I've got to get some sleep," he said. "I'm going out in a few hours to help with the night watch. And Fiana, too," he added, smiling at his wife. "Sorry we can't cook breakfast, Ember. I'm sure Gittel will find something for you to eat!"

"Speaking of food," Gittel said with a laugh, "shall we just have breakfast *now*?"

Ember's eyes brightened and she nodded eagerly. She had hardly eaten anything all day, and Gittel's pancakes were delicious. Gittel's mother gave the girls a goodnight hug, and soon the smell of pancakes and fresh maple syrup filled the air.

" ... and she almost went in the river?" Gittel was saying as she flipped a pancake high into the air, catching it again without even looking as it landed with a plop in the pan. "I don't know if I could have kept on going after that!" she said.

Before long they were sitting at the kitchen table, talking about the storm and the search while they feasted on the towering stack of pancakes.

"One more on top and the whole thing will fall!" Ember joked, giving the stack a nudge with her fork.

"We don't have to eat them all!" Gittel laughed. "I made extra for my parents to have before they go."

"I guess we *could* leave them one or two," Ember said with a grin.

After the meal they went up to Gittel's room, and they lay in their beds talking as the storm rattled the shutters and the thunder rumbled above the rooftops. They talked about Wynton and Merritt, the bears lost out in the storm. About Skye and Merridy, of flying and of books. And they talked about their friends who were already out on Adventure: Growly and Ash and the other boy Cubs.

"What will you do, Gittel, on *your* Adventure?" Ember asked, looking across the room at her friend. She could see the rich, honey brown fur of Gittel's head by the lamplight.

Gittel smiled and was quiet for a moment as she thought. "I'm going to cook," she said with a grin. "Pancakes and applesauce over an open fire."

"I'll be at your camp every morning!" Ember joked. "I wouldn't be able to finish *my* Adventure, but it would almost be worth it for a feast like that!"

"The whole summer, all alone ... " Gittel said quietly. "Ember, do you think we can do it?"

Ember didn't say anything for a moment. To complete an Adventure, a Cub had to be out in the wild for the whole summer. They were not allowed to talk to another bear. At the end of the summer, they would come back from their Adventures, no longer bear Cubs. They would come back as Young Bears. It was a tradition that had been around since before the time of Hegel.

"The whole summer alone," Ember said quietly. Exhaustion was washing over her, and it was getting hard to keep her eyes open. " ... we can do it, Gittel," she whispered, and she drifted off to sleep.

9
Into the Air

There was a muffled pounding downstairs, and at first Ember thought it was just another boom of thunder. She lay there quietly in the darkness, and it took a moment for her to remember she was in the spare bed at Gittel's place. There was that sound again, echoing up the stairs through the stillness.

Stillness?

Ember sat up in bed and looked around. The window shutters were no longer creaking, and the howl of the storm was gone.

"Gittel! Ember!" The sound of Skye's voice called from downstairs. "The storm is over. Wake up!"

Ember quickly dressed in her climbing pants and a sweater and hurried downstairs, with Gittel close behind. Skye was waiting for them in the hall, dressed for flying with her emergency pack on her back.

"The whole village is awake!" she panted. "We'll be taking off at first light, Ember. That's less than an hour away."

Ember nodded and began to pull on her boots.

"I'll get some breakfast," Gittel said as Ember tightened the straps on her pack. "Apples and last night's pancakes, I'm afraid." She grinned, a little embarrassed. "With no syrup, we can eat them on the way."

Soon the three of them were jogging down the main street in the darkness. The sound of activity filled the village as shutters were opened and lamps were lit. As they neared the Lookout, Ember glanced back to see the streets were filling with bears, all carrying lamps and packs, ready to search in the Lower Lands.

"The others are already on the way to Glider Leap," Skye said, as they began the climb up the mountain. "I told them to go on ahead. We can't all take off at once."

"What's your area?" Ember asked Skye, panting as they hurried up the steep path. Her legs were aching, but she hardly noticed.

"I've got the east side of the Lower Woods and down past the Cascade. What about you?"

"I'm on the west," Ember replied. "Starting where you almost went swimming the night before last."

Gittel giggled, and Skye looked at Ember and grinned.

As they reached Glider Leap, the first hint of sunlight could be seen on the horizon—a faint glow in the east that would soon bathe the mountains in red and gold. There were bears up on the landing platform of the Leap.

Glider Leap was one of the oldest buildings in Haven. It had been built when the bears still lived in caves on the side of the mountain. Before the Explorers came. Before there were houses. Hegel and the bears of his time had built the Leap, a small, round building that looked a little like a fortress, with parapet walls of rough, unfinished stone. Glider Leap sat in a narrow valley between the Ears, the two peaks at the top of Mount Hegel, looking northward over the Backlands and south toward The Precipice. Below the landing platform were the storage rooms, filled with gliders and equipment and stacked jars of honey from the Honey Well.

The girl Cubs made their way inside, and with Gittel's help they soon had their bundled gliders up on the platform. The other three pilots were already hard at work, unfolding their gliders and locking the poles in place. They looked up for a moment at the sound of the girls, calling a quick greeting before getting right back to the preparations. Light was stretching out along The Precipice. It was almost time to go. One of the Young Bears leapt to his feet, and Gittel ran over to help him get fastened into his harness. Gittel didn't like flying, but she was an expert assistant. Every pilot loved it when Gittel was there to help.

"I'm going out!" he called, and the next moment he was running down the platform and leaping into the dimness. He began to circle back around, getting lift from the updraft over the Backlands and going higher and higher.

"I'm going out!" called the next pilot, and soon there were two gliders in the air, circling their way upward above Glider Leap.

Ember and Skye were almost ready as a third bear ran down the platform and leapt out over the Backland Valley. Gittel ran back and forth between them, checking bindings and helping lock the poles in place. Everything was always double-checked, and then checked again, just to be sure. There had been a few glider accidents in the history of Haven, but never because of faulty equipment. Every Cub was taught the importance of a careful safety check.

"I'm going out!" Skye called, her face beaming in a wide grin. She had her flight goggles on, but Ember was sure she could see the sparkle in her friend's eyes.

"Skye belongs in the sky," Merridy would say. *"I'm surprised she hasn't grown feathers!"*

"I just might one day, Miss Merridy," Skye would laugh. *"One day I just might."*

Ember tugged on the bindings of her harness again. Everything looked good.

Gittel nodded and gave Ember a smile. "Be careful," she said quietly, steadying the glider as Ember turned and took off at a run down the platform.

There was the sound of the thump of Ember's boots on the stone and the sound of the thump of her heartbeat in her ears, and then the wind caught the wings of the glider and she leapt out into the sky. Wind whistled around her, humming past the wings of the glider as she lifted higher. The others were already diving toward the Lower Lands, speeding over the mountain cliffs and over the rooftops of Haven. Bears in the street cheered as the dark shadows swooped by, the wings of the gliders catching the first beams of morning light.

Ember turned and made a final pass over Glider Leap. Gittel stood waving on the platform, just like Ember had done when Growly left just a few days before. How long ago that seemed now. The storm felt like it had gone on for weeks!

Pushing the nose of the glider down a little, Ember rushed toward Haven, taking a turn over the Lookout tower and then gliding along above the village and out over the Little Cliffs. At the bottom of the cliffs, a wide band of foothills stretched south toward The Precipice, disappearing into a thick stretch of forest called the Lower Woods. South past the woods were more low hills, cut by the twisting torrent of the Cascade River. Beyond that were more hills, and in those hills a little hidden valley, and in that valley sat an ancient cottage. It was Growly's cottage now, at least it would be when he returned from his Adventure. She wondered if maybe one day they might live there ... one day ..."

Ember shook her head and tried to get her focus back on flying. She was smiling though. Growly ... she already missed him.

Ember could see a long line of bears making their way down the steep path toward the Lower Lands. Others were gathered there already, standing on the slopes above the woods as Farren gave them maps and directions. Every bear who could would be out searching today.

Ember whooshed down over the crowd, and then, turning sharply to the right, she caught an updraft and made her way out toward the west. In the distance she could see Skye's glider, making long, arching turns as she searched for the two missing bears.

Coming toward the Cascade River, Ember pulled the glider into a slow turn. This was her search area, out over the Banks.

She flipped down the binoculars attached to her flight cap, a small pair of lenses that looked a lot like flying goggles. It was not safe to fly with them all the time, but once you leveled out they could be used to search. Ember peered down at the churning Cascade and all along the riverbank on either side, pulling back the lenses after a while so she could see a wider area. The Lower Lands were awash with morning light now, and Ember could see the rolling hills and the swirling clouds out beyond The Precipice. Ahead of her lay the Banks, the land beyond the Cascade—clumps of forest and rocky hills all the way to the Great River.

10
Rescue

The Cascade River was in full flood. Ember had never seen the waters so high and so wild. It thundered its way though the Lower Lands, racing and tumbling toward The Precipice. The river had overflowed its banks in many places, making swirling, muddy lakes amongst the trees and sending branching streams out into the meadows.

Ember flew in twisting circles, following the torrent as it headed south and scanning the riverbanks for any sign of the lost bears. She had been searching for over an hour, gazing down through the binoculars for a while and then circling upward on the wind. The shadow of her glider raced along below her, speeding over the countryside in the bright morning sunlight. She was watching it for a moment when she suddenly saw another shadow, speeding over the ground to the left, heading right toward hers.

"A glider!" The thought flashed through her mind and she spun around in panic, trying to see the other glider as she fumbled with the binoculars. Suddenly, a large object whooshed past the wing of her glider. There was a screeching cry, and then whatever it was fell out of sight for a moment, leaving Ember gasping and her heart pounding wildly. "Wha ..."

There was a flash of brown and gold just below her, and Ember's face beamed happily as she realized who it was. "Goldentail!" she cried, calling out to the eagle racing along just below. The eagle let out another cry, glancing up toward her with a sparkle in his eye.

"Goldentail!" Ember shouted again. "You just about scared me out of my glider!"

Goldentail didn't answer. Eagles didn't speak Bear, of course, and bears didn't speak Eagle. Even Merridy couldn't figure out a single Eagle word, and she was better at language than any bear in Haven.

Eagles were smart though. Ember was sure of that. She had flown with them many times, up amongst the cliffs of the Backland Valley. Eagles talked with each other and built sprawling nest homes up in the heights. They knew the weather even better than the bees and were wise and majestic, even when they played. Goldentail was the friendliest of them all. He often flew beside Ember, soaring playfully around her glider on trips to the Honey Well. Now though, there was a determined glint in his eye, as if he knew what was happening and was there to help. He flew up beside Ember and gazed calmly at her for a moment, then let out another shrieking cry as he sped off ahead.

They flew along the course of the river for a while, Goldentail circling and turning, with Ember close behind. Bears were out in the Lower Lands, and gliders were in the air. The eagle knew something was wrong, that the bears were out searching for something. He scanned the ground below, looking for anything out of place, for some sign of movement or flash of color. Suddenly he let out a cry, looking back at Ember before diving toward the ground.

Ember pushed the nose of her glider forward, following Goldentail downward. The eagle had seen something. She just knew it.

There was a thick clump of trees just below, surrounded by low, rocky hills. There were caves in the hills, and Ember suddenly saw a flicker of waving red down amongst the boulders. "Merritt!" Ember cried. Even from this high she could see it was a Cub. But she was all alone! Where was Wynton?

Ember pushed the glider into a tighter dive, looking around frantically for a place to land. There were no open fields nearby, just trees and the open rocks. That would have to do. She swooped low above the treetops, looking down at little Merritt. "I'm coming!" she cried, and Merritt waved her arms excitedly, flapping the bright red scarf she held in her paw.

As she came close to the hills, Ember pulled back on the glider, pushing the nose upward and slowing her speed. "Time it right, Ember!" she whispered to herself, watching the rocky terrain until she saw an open area. With a final pull she plunged her feet down, almost toppling as she landed and came to a stop. In a moment, Ember had the harness unfastened and was scrambling to get the glider secured before a gust of wind could carry it away.

"Ember! Ember, is it you?"

Ember could hear Merritt's cry from just down the hill.

"I'm coming Merritt!" she answered. "Are you OK?" Bounding down the slope, Ember soon saw the little Cub, scrambling her way up the hill.

"Where is Wynton?" Ember gasped, throwing her arms around the frightened Cub. "Are you hurt, Merritt?"

Merritt shook her head. "I'm fine, but Poppy's hurt, Ember. He fell trying to get us back across the river."

Ember held the trembling Cub close. "Where is your poppy?" Ember asked kindly, looking calmly at Merritt.

The little girl Cub lifted a trembling arm, pointing toward a narrow cave over near the trees.

"We stayed in there, Ember. It kept us safe from the storm. Poppy's pack was lost in the river, and we couldn't make a fire. He isn't well, Ember. He's been asleep for a long time."

Ember leapt to her feet and raced toward the cave, pulling off her backpack as she ran. Wynton was just inside, unconscious and burning up with fever. There was a bad break in his leg. Ember could see it right away. He needed the doctor. Soon.

Ember hurried back outside, calling to Merritt as she raced toward the trees. "We need to make a signal fire, Merritt! Get all the sticks and branches you can find!"

It wasn't long before they had a pile of branches out on the rocks. "It's mostly wet!" Ember said to Merritt. She struck her piece of flint and sent a little shower of sparks down onto her fire kit: oil soaked rags and sticks dipped in wax. All the bears of the Rescue Committee carried a fire kit in their emergency packs. In a moment Ember had a small fire blazing. "Now for the smoke," she said to Merritt with a wink.

The little Cub grinned. Everything felt a little better now that help was here.

Ember began to toss green, leafy branches onto the fire, sending a thick plume of smoke up into the sky. "It won't be long," she said with a smile. "They're watching for smoke signals. There are bears out searching all over the Lower Lands."

"Look!" gasped Merritt, jumping to her feet and pointing up into the sky. Goldentail circled above the river, and just beyond him a glider was racing down toward them.

"Skye!" Ember shouted happily as she saw the markings on the glider.

In a moment, Skye whooshed over their heads and swooped down for a landing.

"Where is Wynton?" Skye cried, looking around as she noticed the older bear wasn't there.

"He's hurt, Skye," Ember said, trying to hide the concern in her voice. "I hope the others get here soon. He needs the doctor."

Sky looked alarmed. "The bridge, Ember!" she gasped. "The riverbanks on this side are flooded. I could see it from the air.

"I saw some of the flooding, too," Ember said seriously, trying to think of what to do next. "How wide is the flooding?" she asked. "Could we swim to the bridge?"

Skye shook her head. "It looks deep, Ember. And it's flowing fast. It's too far to throw a rope across. I don't know how they'll reach us."

Ember sat in silence for a moment, desperately trying to think of what to do.

"Maybe ... " An idea was starting to form. Ember suddenly grabbed her pack and pulled out the long length of rope stored in the bottom. "Forty feet," she mumbled, "and with yours that makes eighty." She looked up at Skye with a grin. "Do you think you can take off from the top of that hill?"

An hour later, Ember and Merritt stood beside the river, looking out across the churning water to the bridge. The path on this side was cut off by the flood, and way out in the middle of the Cascade, the sturdy stone bridge came to a sudden end. Fergal was out on the bridge, and other bears of the Rescue Committee, too. They were desperately trying to find a way to get across the wide, flowing torrent ahead of them.

"OK, Skye," Ember whispered. "Oh, please let this work." She looked up toward the hills and waved Merritt's bright red scarf. There was a sudden movement on the hilltop, and Skye's glider lifted up into the air, speeding over the treetops toward Ember.

"Not yet!" Ember gasped as Skye raced down toward them. "Ready ... and ... NOW!" she cried, and she threw the scarf into the air. Suddenly a small rock hurtled out and away from the glider. It was tied to a long length of rope. Ember leapt into action, racing toward the rock and diving for the rope before it was pulled into the river. "Got it!" she cried, and Merritt let out a happy cheer.

The rope trailed out behind the glider, stretching across the water as Skye headed right for the bridge.

"The rope!" Farren's shout could be heard across the water. "Grab the rope!"

There was movement on the bridge, and then a loud cheer.

Ember's face beamed. She scrambled over to a nearby tree and tied her end firmly around the trunk. She waved to Farren, and in a moment the long rope was pulled tight.

"We're coming to get you!" Farren called, as bears on the bridge tightened the rope and prepared to cross.

Ember felt her legs begin to wobble, and she let out a loud sigh of relief as she plopped down on the soft grass of the riverbank.

"We did it," Merritt whispered. There were tears in her eyes, and she threw her arms around Ember's neck and snuggled up in her lap.

11
The Day

Ember woke to the sound of Merridy's voice, soft and joyful as she came into the bedroom. "It's today, Ember! The sun is coming up. I thought you would want to see it."

Ember's eyes opened wide and her heart began to pound with excitement as she leapt out of bed and threw her arms around Merridy.

"It's today!" she gasped. Letting go of Merridy, she scrambled over to her backpack. "Do you think I've forgotten anything, Mama? Oh ... I know I've forgotten *something*!"

Merridy laughed softly. "You've forgotten to give me another hug. I need all of them I can get. Oh Ember, I'm going to miss you!"

It had been two days now since the rescue. It took Farren and his team a while to get Wynton and Merritt across the flooded river to the bridge. More ropes were strung out over the water, and they had to build a raft to carry the injured bear. Ember held her breath the whole time they pulled him across, though he was surrounded by rescuers and the raft was tied firmly. Merritt went with him, and when they were safely on the bridge, Ember waved goodbye and went back to her glider. She had climbed the hill, just as Skye did, and took off from there, spiraling into the sky on the updrafts until she was high enough to return to Glider Leap. When she finally made it home to the library, it was early afternoon. She had fallen into bed and slept right through till the following morning.

She had spent the day yesterday checking on Wynton and Merritt and helping with repairs in the village. Wynton was already improving. His fever was gone, and he joked with Ember and asked her to sign the cast on his leg. "Last time I go swimming in a flooded river," he joked with a smile and a groan. Then he had said seriously, "Thank you, Ember."

There was some damage in Haven from the storm. Torn-off shutters and a few broken windows. Even a door that had completely blown away. But no bears (other than Wynton, of course) had been injured. Merridy had flown out to the Honey Well and spent an hour watching the bees. They would signal if any of the Cubs out on Adventure in the mountain valleys had been hurt. Bees had a language all their own—a kind of dance and movement the bear, Hegel, had discovered centuries ago. Merridy knew the Bee language better than anyone in

Haven. She and her friend, C.J., had studied it together back before he was lost over The Precipice.

"No Cubs injured," she had reported as she returned to the village. "And no damage to the Honey Well either."

And now it was *the day*! Ember looked around her bedroom and took a deep breath. "Goodbye, comfy bed!" she said with a laugh. "Oh Merridy! I can hardly wait!"

"I have breakfast ready for you down in the library," the older bear said. "I thought it might be fun to eat in front of the big windows, to look down at where you'll be spending the next few months." Merridy turned and started to make her way into the hall. "Make sure you get dressed before you come down. You never know who might drop by this morning to wish you well."

Ember pulled on her clothes. *Adventure* clothes for today. Hiking pants and a long sleeve shirt. She had a couple of dresses packed, even if she *was* going to be out in the woods. Today though, she wanted to look like an adventurer.

She made her way quickly down the stairs, stepping lightly in the early morning dimness as she came into the hallway that led to the library.

"Gittel? Skye!" Ember gasped, almost bumping into her two friends.

"Merridy said she wanted to give us something," Gittel said, sounding rather puzzled.

"She came by my place, too!" Skye added.

"Probably for a breakfast together," Ember said, "to say goodbye before we leave."

They slowly made their way into the main library room. Walking carefully in the darkness. "Merridy ... ?"

"SURPRISE!" There was a sudden burst of light and a deafening cheer as lamps were uncovered, and Ember saw the library was full of bears. Growly's parents, Farren and Edolie. And his grandparents, Fergal and Mika. Gittel's mother and father, and Skye's too, with her little brother, Dugan. And gathered all around, a room full of friends and relatives who had come to say goodbye to the three girl Cubs.

The sun was coming up over the Lower Lands, filling the library with a warm, orange glow. One by one the bears turned out their lamps, and the sound of laughter and talking quieted for a moment as they all gazed out the tall library windows at the sunrise. It was a beautiful sight. Beams of light stretched over the Lower Lands, pushing back the shadows and bathing the meadows in crimson and gold. And The Precipice! It was always magnificent. The jagged cliff edge stretched as far as one could see to the west and the east. It was the edge of the world, as far as the bears knew. Only one bear had gone over it, and he never returned. There were only clouds beyond The Precipice, stretching off toward the horizon like a thick carpet, streaked with the deep purples and reds of the sunrise.

"Isn't it beautiful this morning!" Ember whispered, taking Merridy's paw in hers.

Merridy only nodded. She was staring out toward The Precipice, and there were tears in the corners of her eyes.

Just then, there was a call from the doorway that led to Gittel's house. "Make way! Breakfast is here!" Gittel's mother bustled into the room carrying an enormous tray piled high with towers of pancakes.

Adwin was right behind her, carrying another tray. "Pancakes with the sunrise! There is nothing better!" he said with a laugh. "Unless, of course, you throw in a good cup of tea."

There was a long table in the center of the room, and soon it was loaded with even more food. The bears crowded around it, filling their plates with breakfast while the room rang with the sound of laughter and song. There were speeches, of course, and Fergal had everyone howling with stories of Farren as a Cub.

Growly's father shook his head. "Did I really do *that* when I was little?" He groaned, looking over at his mother, Mika.

Mika smiled. "Fergal," she scolded, looking lovingly at her husband, "that wasn't *exactly* how it happened!"

"Oh?" said Fergal, pretending to look surprised.

"Yes," said Mika, "he didn't just run out into the street in a towel. He also had a bucket on his head! He was shouting as he ran because he liked the sound it made!"

Everyone roared with laughter, especially Farren. He could vaguely remember doing something like that.

"I should try that again!" he said, when the laughter had calmed a little. "It *was* a really wonderful sound!" There was another roar of laughter, and Skye's father almost choked on his tea, coughing and spluttering as he pounded the table and wiped a happy tear from his eye.

"Enough about my cubhood," Farren said with a smile as the room calmed down again. He stood up next to the table and raised his mug of tea in the air. "One last speech, and then we must get ready to go to the Lookout." He turned to Ember then, his voice a little shaky as he quietly continued, "Ember, you are truly a gift to the village of Haven. From the moment you were found, you have brought joy and wonder to us all. We are proud of you, and we love you. I know that any bear in Haven would say the same."

There was silence for a moment—just the sound of a sniffle as Merridy nodded and wiped away a tear—and then the room erupted again with shouts and cheers as the bears went off to get ready for the day.

12
Adventure Ember, Adventure

The bears of Haven were gathered at the Lookout, spread out around the enormous rock on which the tower was built. The air was filled with the sounds of laughter and the shouts of the younger Cubs all mixed in with the buzz of excited conversation.

Suddenly the mayor appeared, up on the ledge at the foot of the Lookout. He was dressed, as he did on important occasions, in his top hat and coat. His voice boomed loudly and seriously out over the crowd, "Bears of Haven ..."

Ember was already grinning. It was the same speech every time a bear went out on Adventure.

"Would you join me in singing 'The Ode to Bartholomew the Brown'?"

Some of the little Cubs giggled hysterically. They knew what was coming next.

"No!" shouted all the bears, shaking their heads as the mayor did his best to look serious.

"Well, what shall we sing then?" he called.

"Sing an Adventure song!" everyone shouted, and they burst into song, some with paws over their hearts, some swinging their arms in the air. All the bears sang with all their might and tried their best to hold back the laughter.

It was "Adventure My Bear, Adventure," of course. That was always the song they sang. It was the silliest of all the Adventure songs—and the most loved. They had sung it just days ago when Growly and Ash left for their Adventures. And they would sing it again in the following days as other Cubs went out for the summer. It was tradition, and it was one that never felt old.

Ember looked over at Gittel and Skye as they joyfully sang along with the crowd, stretching out the final line of the chorus until everyone howled with laughter. Ember had sung the song hundreds of times, and she always loved it. Today though, she could feel an excitement bubbling up inside her that made every silly line of the song seem special and important.

As the last notes echoed around her, she was surprised to feel tears welling in the corners of her eyes. She had to take a deep breath to try to hold them back. The song had felt different this time. The song had felt like family and friends and of history and belonging. The song had felt like ... home.

"Bears ... are there some Adventurers here today?"

"Skye!" shouted the bears all together, and then, "Gittel ... Ember!"

There was another loud cheer, but Ember hardly even heard. She was lost in her thoughts.

"Ember," Merridy whispered, giving her daughter a nudge with her elbow.

Ember blinked in surprise and looked around.

"Adventure Ember, ADVENTURE!" called the mayor with a laugh from up on the platform.

Gittel and Skye were already halfway up the stairs that led to the base of the Lookout, and they turned and smiled when they saw their friend, still down in the crowd looking a little bewildered.

"You've got the whole summer to daydream!" Gittel called with a giggle.

Ember laughed, shaking her head, and raced up the stairs after her two friends.

Soon they were all standing next to the mayor, looking down at the crowd below.

"These are three fine bears," the mayor announced, giving the Cubs a wink. "They will leave here today as Cubs, but when they return, they will be Young Bears."

The crowd cheered.

"Skye," he continued, "I know it will be hard to be away from your glider, but please don't try flapping your arms and jumping out of trees!"

There was a roar of laughter from the crowd, and Skye did a little bow, her eyes sparkling. She leaned closer to the mayor. "I just might!" she whispered with a grin.

The mayor chuckled and shook his head. "And Gittel! If it weren't for the rules and traditions, we'd all be down at your campsite for supper every night!"

Gittel smiled and gave the mayor a big, joyous hug.

"Ember," the mayor said finally, "the Lower Woods will be a brighter place with you in it, but please hurry back! You know how mischievous Fergal, Mika, and Merridy get when you're not there to keep them in their place!" He said the last sentence extra loudly, giving Merridy a playful wave as the bears of the village roared with more laughter.

"Travel well," he said softly to the three girl Cubs. "We'll see you at the end of the summer."

Then, turning back to the gathered bears he called, "Three cheers for the Adventurers!"

<hr />

There were farewells then, and a noisy parade down the main street as the three friends made their way through Haven. Merritt walked along proudly between Ember and Gittel. Skye's little brother, Dugan, clung to his sister's paw and looked shyly up at the cheering crowd as they came to the end of the village.

"Write down everything!" Merridy said with a sniffle, as she gave her daughter another hug. "I want to hear *everything* as soon as you return. Oh, my dear Ember. I will miss you!"

"Don't worry, Mama," Ember said with a smile. "The summer will fly by, and I know you will have plenty of fun with Fergal and Mika. And plenty of mischief!"

"I probably will!" Merridy laughed.

Then, after one last hug, Ember and her two friends waved farewell to the cheering crowd and started their way down toward the Lower Lands.

⸭⸭⸭⸭⸭⸭⸭⸭⸭⸭⸭⸭⸭⸭⸭⸭⸭

"Did you pack your whole kitchen, Gittel?" Skye asked with a laugh as they came panting down the path at the foot of the Little Cliffs. "Your pack looks like it weighs a ton!"

"A ton and a half!" Gittel chuckled. "And I have to travel the farthest!" She wiped her face with the sleeve of her shirt, bouncing the heavy weight of the pack on her back. "I didn't bring *much* from my kitchen. Just my favorite pancake skillet and three small pots," she grinned, "and some ladles and whisks ... but not much more than that!"

Ember laughed. "What about you, Skye? Do you manage to squeeze your glider in there?"

"I wish!" Skye giggled. "No, mine is mostly food. Things I won't be able to find in the wild, like cake and muffins and other essential things. The woods are not a place to go without a good supply of sweet baked deliciousness. Of course I did pack other things I might need, too."

"Like chocolate!" Gittel added, and the three friends burst into giggles again as they made their way down through the foothills toward the forest.

"This is where we leave you," Skye said with a quiet smile, as they reached the edge of the trees.

Ember nodded and sighed. "I'll miss you both so much!" she said softly, putting her arms around her friends' shoulders as they stood for a moment on the path. "See you at the end of the summer," she whispered, and then her friends were on their way, continuing down the path across the open meadows. Ember watched until they were out of sight. "See you at the end of the summer," she whispered again, suddenly noticing the silence and the stillness all around her.

"Adventure Ember, Adventure," she said to herself with a shaky smile, and she made her way off the rocky path and into the Lower Woods.

13
The Lower Woods

As the forest closed in around her, Ember entered a world of shadows and bright beams of sunlight, piercing down though the leafy branches of the trees. Towering oaks and maples creaked in the brisk mountain breeze, and the sound of rustling leaves and birdcalls filled the air.

Ember stood still for a moment, listening and breathing in the familiar smell of the forest. She loved it here. She always had. For as far back as Ember could remember, Merridy had taken her exploring in the Lower Woods. Through thick, tickling patches of fern and under the swaying evergreen pines. By streams and open meadows. It had always been a place of wonder to her. And now, here she was on her Adventure. A whole summer alone amongst the trees.

Ember took a deep breath and grinned. There would be lonely times ahead—she knew that. But right now she felt as light as a feather and tingling with excitement. A squirrel chattered noisily up above, and there was the sound of a woodpecker somewhere in the distance. Behind it all was the whistle of the wind as it blew through the tops of the branches on its way toward Haven.

As she moved deeper into the forest, the trees became taller and the undergrowth thicker. Ember found herself pushing through dense patches of fern that came up above her waist. She knew this part of the forest well. *The Whispering Way.* That's what Growly called it. A place where the ferns grew so tall they went right over your head, and if you whispered no one could tell where you were. Grown up bears, of course, could see the rustling of the ferns, but they always acted surprised when the Cubs leapt out of the leaves with a shout.

On the other side of the Whispering Way would be a stream, and on the other side of that began the pines, stretching for half a mile toward the east. Ember hiked through the tall trees, whistling happily as her boots crunched through the pine needles that lay like a carpet under her feet. Past the pines she came to another stretch of oaks and maples—the ground here green with moss and fern, scattered with wildflowers and fallen leaves.

"Almost there!" Ember could feel her heart pounding as she saw the enormous oak tree and heard the familiar rushing chatter of a nearby stream. "Just down the slope and through those trees ..."

Ember burst through a wall of ferns and came out into a narrow meadow. Tall oaks surrounded it, with branches reaching out over the sparkling waters of a deep pond. A stream cut down through the meadow, dashing and twisting its way southward from the mountains to the pond, and then into the forest again on the other side. There was an apple tree farther up the slope and a thick patch of berries down near the river. Ember slipped off her pack and flopped to the ground, stretching out happily on the soft, cool grass and gazing up at the thin wisps of cloud in the sky.

"Home," Ember whispered, and she closed her eyes, enjoying the feeling of the breeze as it tousled the fur around her ears.

She set up camp under the bough of an oak near the pond, pitching her tent on the soft grass and making a circle of stones for a fire pit out by the stream. She made a chair, of sorts, out of branches, sharpened with her hatchet and driven into the soft ground for the back. She even built armrests and a holder for her teacup. There was no sense in being uncomfortable, even if you were living out in the woods.

She hung a clothesline between two low branches and built a fire in the circle of stones. As evening settled over the little meadow, Ember feasted on fire-roasted potatoes and baked apples and then sat back in her chair by the river and sipped a hot mug of tea.

She sat there for a long time, watching the first stars appear in the night sky and listening to the sounds of the forest. Fireflies danced lazily in the summer breeze, filling the meadow with drifting sparkles of light. The dark shadows of the cliffs rose up into the night sky to the north, and above them, the towering peaks at the edge of the Alps. Growly was up there somewhere, and Ash and the other boy Cubs their age, up in the high mountain valleys nestled in amongst the peaks. Growly would probably be sitting by a fire, just like she was. Probably still wearing the same clothes he'd had on when he left. Ember smiled at the thought. And he'd probably be writing something in his journal. Some funny little story or poem or song. Growly loved to write down things, and to doodle and sketch. He got that from his parents, and his grandparents, too.

"He'll be a writer one day," Merridy would often say. "Either that or he'll empty the village of notebooks." Growly had piles of notebooks in his bedroom, and stacks of papers and sketches tied in bundles with string. "He's a *good* bear, Ember." Merridy would often say that. And she always seemed to say it with a smile and a wink. Growly ... Ember smiled now as she thought of him up there in the mountains, all by himself, out on his Adventure. She missed him a lot. It was a strange, happy-sad feeling. Merridy was right. He *was* a good bear.

The sky was bright with stars when Ember finally crawled into her tent, bundling snugly in her sleeping bag as the moon crept up slowly above the tops of the trees. The forest felt peaceful and quiet, though she could always hear the sound of rustling leaves or the creaking of branches and wind in the treetops. Ember lay sleepily in the tent, lulled by the chatter of the stream as it gurgled and splashed out into the pond. The hoot of an owl came from somewhere far off in the forest, its call soft and distant under the sound of frogs and crickets.

Ember turned out her lamp and let the sounds take her gently off to sleep, into dreams filled with mountains and forests and fields. She dreamed of Merridy and Gittel, and of pancakes and storms, and of a Cub with a blue backpack, flying off into the sky. Her heart ached a little as the wind lifted him away. He was *a good bear*.

14
Things to do When You're Camping

Ember crept along through the ferns, staying low and stepping as quietly as she could. It was not that she needed to. All the small animals and birds in the area were used to her by now, and there was no one around to hide from. She was creeping simply because it was fun, and it made everything feel mysterious and exciting.

Crouching low beneath the ferns, Ember carefully pulled the small telescope from her coat pocket, extending it and putting it up to her eye. She pushed the end of the telescope through the ferns, staying as low and hidden as she could.

There they were. Ember let out a happy sigh as she caught sight of a little nest, high up in the branches of a nearby tree. There were two small babies in the nest, chirping excitedly as their mother nestled in between them. Ember had watched them hatch a few weeks ago, and she had been back every day since, noting how their feathers were coming in and guessing at their size. Opening her little journal, Ember wrote down every detail, noting the way the mother fluffed her feathers and doing her best to describe the sound of the babies as they chirped.

With her notes complete, Ember closed the telescope and put it back in her pocket. Then she stood up with a grin, waving up toward the nest. The little birds cheeped with excitement as they saw her appear suddenly amongst the ferns, and the mother bird hopped up on the side of the nest and fluttered down onto Ember's shoulder.

"They're getting so big," Ember whispered to the bird, removing a small piece of bread from her pocket. The mother took it in her beak and gave Ember a nod of thanks before she flew back to the nest. "See you tomorrow!" Ember called, and the babies flapped and chirped joyfully. She wished she could say something in their language. She'd been trying to figure it out for weeks. But no bear had ever learned Bird.

"C.J. tried once," Merridy had said. "But at the time he was more focused on the bees. He came to the conclusion that birds had many languages. At least that's how it seemed. He said someday day he would learn one. That was before he went over The Precipice."

Ember sighed. C.J. had been better at languages than any bear in Haven. If he couldn't learn Bird, it might not be learnable. Still, she was having a great time trying. She wandered for a while amongst the trees, stopping to feast on the berries that grew on tangly bushes and on nuts the squirrels hadn't hidden yet.

As she went along, she stopped from time to time to scribble in her journal or examine some interesting leaf or bug. She climbed up the towering oak that grew down by the meadow, sitting high in the branches as they swayed in the wind. She lay in the soft grass, watching the clouds and making sketches of their shapes and what she imagined them to be. "That one looks like a squirrel riding a wheelbarrow!" Ember giggled, and she was about to start drawing it when she felt a soft, tickly nibble on her foot.

"Squiggle!" she gasped happily, as she looked down and saw the baby rabbit trying to climb up onto her foot. "Where's your mama?"

There was a nudge at her elbow, and Ember turned to see a larger rabbit by her side. "I was wondering where you two were," Ember said with a smile. "It's almost midday, and I was beginning to think I might have to eat my lunch all alone."

The mother rabbit looked up at Ember quietly, as one of her long, fluffy ears gave a twitch.

"Oh, I wish I could speak Rabbit, too," Ember said with a sigh. "I wish I could hear about all you've been doing."

Squiggle had managed to climb up onto Ember's foot, and with a happy squeak he began to wobble his way up toward her knee.

"Come here!" she said, lifting the little rabbit in her paws and feeling his soft fur against her cheek.

Squiggle (as Ember called him) and his mother had been coming to the meadow for the last few weeks. They had been shy at first, but now they came and played happily in the tall grass, nibbling fresh leaves and berries Ember gathered for them in the woods. After lunch they would sit together by the river until it was time for Squiggle and his mother to go back to their burrow.

Other birds and animals came to visit as well, and as the weeks slipped slowly by, Ember almost always had company, and she rarely felt alone. There were times at night though, when the sky bristled with stars and the fire turned into glowing coals, that Ember felt lonely.

"It's the part of your Adventure that really makes it *adventure.*" That's what Merridy would say. "It can't all be sunshine and cupcakes and soft fluffy sleeping bags. *Flowers need to get rained on if they want to grow tall.*"

And Ember did get rained on from time to time. There were days she awoke with the wind howling through the meadow and nights when lightning crackled overhead. At those times she sheltered in caves up by the cliffs, with a blazing fire and a hot mug of tea.

When she wasn't exploring or writing in her journal, Ember spent long hours swimming in the pond and lying out under the warm sun to dry. She built a raft out of branches and logs, and she raced twigs down the tumbling stream. She chased fish in the shallow water, giggling and squealing as she splashed about. She made a rope swing on a thick oak branch. Squirrels and birds gathered to watch her soar out over the water and land with a splash in the middle of the pond. Squiggle and his family loved to come and watch her swing.

She planted wildflowers all along the river and in a circle right around her tent. And she planted daisy seeds out in the meadow. Long rows that spelled out the letters of her name. They were blooming now, and Ember wished she could see them from up high—fluttering white letters in the midst of the wide, green forest.

Her evenings were spent cooking meals over the fire: roasted vegetables and camp bread and grilled nuts and firetop pies. She always finished with a hot cup of tea and reading in her camp chair by the light of her lamp. And so, the weeks slipped happily by, as the summer grew hotter and then began to turn toward fall. Ember marked each day in her journal until finally the time came, and she made ready to leave on the Great Night Hike.

15
The Cub's Adventure Manual

Ember had been mapping out her path for the last few weeks. The Great Night Hike was the toughest part of a girl Cub's Adventure. The boy Cubs had the Nights of Challenge, or "The Great Ice Cave Sleepover," as Growly liked to call it. The girl Cubs would spread out over the Lower Lands, hiking through the nights and sleeping out in the open during the days. They couldn't take any supplies, just a small hiking lamp and a canteen for water.

Ember would head east to the edge of the Lower Woods, and then south all the way to The Precipice, making her way back westward until she came to the hills near the Cascade River. From there, she would head north until she made it to the stone bridge, and back south again until she came to the hidden meadow and Growly's cottage. That would be the first night's hiking. She would sleep during the day down by The Precipice and then head northwest the next night, up into the Banks and along the shore of the Great River. She would travel for three nights in all, ending up back in the little meadow once again in the heart of the Lower Woods.

It wasn't important where a girl Cub traveled during The Great Night Hike. The only rules were that she must hike all night, every night. The only food she could take was three pieces of chocolate, three sandwiches, three apples, and a pocketful of nuts. The rest of her food must be found along the way. Of course she must also do it alone.

Ember loaded everything in her pack, rolling up her tent and tying it with a piece of rope. She would store her things in one of the caves up by the cliffs, just in case there was a heavy storm while she was away on her hike. With everything stowed, Ember took one last look around the meadow, taking in a deep breath as the sunset sparkled on the surface of the pond. "See you in a little while," she whispered, and with darkness settling in around her, she started off into the trees.

When Ember finally reached the end of the forest, the moon was lifting up over the mountains, flooding the Lower Lands in a silvery glow. Ember looked out over the rolling meadows to a stretch of low hills in the distance. There were more woods on the other side of the hills, and beyond that, The Precipice. Ember looked up at the open sky, clear and bright with sparkling stars. There would be no rain tonight. That was a relief.

"*The Great Night Hike must continue under all conditions … except of course bad storms, lightning, or heavy hail.*" That's what *The Cub's Adventure Manual* said. Older versions of the book had also included blizzards, but that had been removed in recent years since no bear could recall there ever being a blizzard in the summer. "*Girl Cubs must hike from dark until dawn, stopping only for ten minute breaks every two hours. A girl Cub may pause for a sip of water at any time, but she may not stop for a sandwich until the midnight hour, at which time she may eat said sandwich as well as a paw-full of nuts and one apple.*" The manual was very specific when it came to the night hike, especially about food. "*One piece of chocolate is allowed each night … but only one. And it must be eaten while lying down and tapping your boots together.*" No one had any idea when that last line was added, or who added it, or why. But it was in the manual and so it was the way that it must be done. Bears took Adventure traditions very seriously.

Ember set off into the meadows, whistling as she pushed through the long grass, which came up above her waist. She held her lamp out as she went, carefully watching with each step for rocks or hidden holes. She crossed over the dusty path that led through the Lower Lands. Gittel and Skye were somewhere out there, miles off to the east in the patches of forest that ran along the foot of the mountains. They would be out hiking tonight, too, trying not to fall in holes, and at some point, lying down and eating a piece of chocolate while tapping their boots together. Ember smiled.

"A girl Cub may hum while she is hiking, but only an Adventure song. She may also whistle, but not while eating her sandwich or lying down for chocolate." The girl Cubs had all giggled when Merridy read the rules to them in the library. *The Cub's Adventure Manual* was full of funny rules and customs.

"They're part of what makes your Adventure special," Merridy had told them. "Once you've been on your Adventure you'll always eat chocolate with a grin."

"I already do!" Skye had said excitedly, and that had gotten every one laughing.

"Silly traditions can be just as important as serious ones," Merridy had said. "It's the silly traditions you'll laugh about with your children, like a funny story we're all a part of. It's the silly traditions that often feel the most like home."

Ember smiled as she thought back on the conversation. They had laughed together for hours, reading about *"songs to sing while washing a plate"* or *"rules for swimming after rolling in mud."*

"Did you do all those things?" Ember had asked Merridy through the giggles.

"Oh yes!" Merridy had replied, wiping away tears from the laughing. "And this was my favorite," she added, pointing to another section and reading it out loud to the girl Cubs. "*Rules for eating apple pan pies without using your paws.*" Merridy grinned at the memory. "Very sticky ... and very fun!"

It was true. Over the past weeks, Ember had worked her way through the manual, following every instruction and laughing all the way. Silly traditions could be a *lot* of fun.

She was almost at the hills now, and the grass became shorter and the ground more rocky. Ember made her way carefully along, holding the lamp out in front of her as the land began to rise. The moon hung bright above her, lighting the terrain. But it also cast deep night shadows where it would be easy to trip.

"*Main Rule for the Great Night Hike,*" Ember said to herself, remembering the title from *The Cub's Adventure Manual.*

"*Watch where you are going!* ...

Do not:

1. Fall in hole, or any other place that could cause injury.

2. Trip on rock, stump, log, forest animal, etc.

3. Fall in river (unless it is a hot night).

4. Run with your eyes closed, even if it feels exciting. (This line was added centuries ago, after a Cub ran right into a tree.)

5. Throw your lamp high into the air and try to catch it—it's just common sense."

That's how the manual went. It kept growing through the years as more sections were added. Some of it was serious, and a lot of it was funny. And all the bears kept their copies in a special place, even when they were grown up and had Cubs of their own. It was a precious reminder of their time on Adventure, and it was wonderful reading when you needed a smile.

"Almost time for my chocolate break," Ember thought, looking up at the moon as she neared the crest of a hill. She grinned. She had only been going for a few hours. Her chocolate break wasn't scheduled till long after midnight. She was planning to lie in the soft grass of the hidden meadow and watch the first glow of morning. She would sleep by the Cascade, just out of sight of Growly's cottage, in a cave by the river they had played in when they were little.

"A Cub must be ready for sleep at the first light of morning and must stay hidden in her sleeping place till the sun fully sets." That's how it was written in the manual.

Ember drew in a deep breath as she reached the top of the hill and looked out to the south at a long stretch of darkness that fell into clouds. The sixth main rule for hiking was suddenly running through her head:

"Remember:

6. When hiking near The Precipice, DO NOT get close to the edge."

16
A Night by The Precipice

The Precipice stretched off into the darkness on her left and right as Ember gazed out over clouds below. They continued as far as she could see in the moonlight, a swirling, silvery blanket all the way to the horizon.

"It's the edge of the world," some bears said, but most believed there must be something out there below the clouds. What it was though was just a guess. Only one bear had gone out over The Precipice, and he had never returned.

It was many years ago. Before Ember had been found by the Great River. Back when Growly's father Farren was just a little Cub. Merridy had told her the story many times. She knew it better than anyone. "I waved goodbye to him up on Glider Leap," she had said. "We were so young ... not much older than you are now, Ember. Off on his Adventure for the summer. C.J. is younger than I am, Ember. I had done my Adventure the year before. We would have been married if he hadn't gone missing.

"'When I get back, I'll ask you to marry me.' That's the way he proposed," Merridy remembered with a far away smile.

"And what did you say to him, Mama?" Ember asked, even though she'd heard it many times before.

"'Then I'll be waiting, Crispin Jacoby.' That's the last thing I said. The bears of Haven searched along the edge of The Precipice for many years, looking for a way down—for any sign of C.J. It was years later when the bird appeared—the little blue and red bird that came to the library window. It tapped C.J.'s signal, the knock he always made when he came to visit, and it had a message. Three words it showed me in the language of the bees. 'Alive. Searching. Love.' There was no mistaking when I saw it, Ember. Only C.J. could teach a bird to move in the language of bees."

C.J. was out there. Ember was sure of it, too. Now, after all these years, the little bird had returned. Merridy had seen it, and so had Growly and Ember. Up on Glider Leap right before Growly left in his glider. "Where are you?" Ember whispered, looking out into the night. With a sigh she turned and started off again westward.

It was well after midnight when she came to the stone bridge that stretched out over the Cascade River toward the western part of the Lower Lands, the region near the Great River called the Banks. There had been much work on the bridge over the past weeks since the storm.

Sandbags held back most of the flooding water, and the bridge had been extended farther to reach the higher ground. The Cascade River thundered underneath, still much higher than Ember had ever seen it. The spray from the river felt fresh and cool against her cheek, with the smell of the high mountains, of ice caves and snow. It made her think of Growly and his Nights of Challenge. He'd be up in an ice cave right now, bundled in his sleeping bag and wearing three pairs of socks. It was not too bad though.

"Boy Cubs may wear all the clothes they have during the Nights of Challenge," The Cub's Adventure Manual stated. *"And they may bundle in blankets and sleeping bags and towels. They may eat what they like, though the food must be cold. And, of course, chocolate must be eaten while lying on your back."*

"It's not the cold that makes the Nights of Challenge a challenge," Farren would say. "The challenge is just for a boy Cub to stay in one place for three days."

Yes, Growly would be just fine, and he wouldn't get bored up there in the cold. He'd come down with a new story in one of his notebooks. He probably wouldn't even notice that three nights had gone by.

The path on the other side of the bridge turned southward again toward The Precipice. Ember picked up her pace, almost jogging as she came through a narrow pass in the hills and into a small patch of woods. Dawn was only an hour away, and the moon was already low over the mountains. She had to hurry if she was going to make it to the river cave by morning. Pausing amongst the trees, Ember turned out her lamp, peeking through the leaves toward the valley up ahead. There was a dim glow coming from just over a rise, and in the faint light Ember could see a thin wisp of smoke twisting up into the night.

Leaving the path, Ember crept quietly through the soft grass of the meadow, staying low as she came over the rise. A short way ahead of her, just past a big oak tree with a rope swing, stood a little cottage, quiet and peaceful in the early morning. There was a light coming from the kitchen window, but Ember couldn't see any movement inside. Still, she couldn't be too careful. Dropping to her knees she crawled through long grass, making her way to the edge of the meadow, where the Cascade River thundered toward The Precipice.

Coming to the banks of the river, Ember stood up again, hidden by darkness and shadows as she crept along. She was halfway down the meadow when she heard the sound of a door opening and voices outside the cottage. Ember dropped down into the grass, her heart pounding. It was still very dark, but what if she had been seen?

"Come on out," said one of the voices.

Ember almost gasped. Her heart was thumping.

"We're coming, we're coming!" said another voice from inside the cottage.

Ember let out a sigh of relief. She hadn't been seen.

"It won't be long till sunrise," said the first voice. She could recognize it now. It was Fergal.

"Oh, it's going to be a beautiful one this morning," said the second voice. It was Mika. "Come on, Merridy. Is the tea almost ready?"

In a moment the three of them appeared, Merridy carrying a tray with steaming mugs as they made their way to the back porch, which looked out toward The Precipice. There was a little more conversation that Ember couldn't quite make out. Something about Fergal needing his beauty sleep that got Merridy and Mika laughing. Then they were quiet for a long moment, sitting back in their rocking chairs and gazing out toward The Precipice.

Ember was just about to continue on her way when she heard Fergal's voice once more, soft but strong and full of emotion.

"To C.J.," he said, raising his steaming mug in a toast. Merridy and Mika nodded. "May you find your way back home, and may you find it soon."

"To C.J.," said Mika, resting a paw on her husband's trembling arm.

"To C.J.," echoed Merridy. "Find your way back soon, Crispin, my love."

Ember felt tears welling in her eyes, and it was all she could do not to run to the cottage and throw her arms around Merridy.

"To C.J.," she whispered, a tear trickling down her cheek. And she turned and crept off toward the cave by the river.

17

Goodbye to the Meadow

Ember sat by the side of the pond, her fur still a little damp from her swim. She had returned to the Lower Woods yesterday, feeling tired and grimy after three nights' walking on the Great Night Hike. She had slept the first day in the cave by the Cascade River, waking just before dusk to continue on her way. Creeping back past the cottage again, she could see lights and hear the sound of voices inside. Oh, how she missed Merridy and Fergal and Mika! How she missed being with all the bears of Haven. Most of her time on Adventure had been wonderful, but two months alone had felt like a *very* long time.

On her second night hiking, she had traveled through the hills west of the Cascade, trekking down through fruit groves and patches of woods into the rugged, rocky wildlands know as the Banks. As she had come down through the hills, she could see the churning torrent of the Great River ahead. Even if it had been daytime she would not have been able to see the other side. This close to the falls, the air above the river was always filled with cloud and spray, blown northward in twisting sheets by the wind from The Precipice.

Ember spent the second day of her hike sleeping in a cave that looked out over the water. It usually would be hard to sleep with the roar of the river rumbling by, but Ember was exhausted and almost as soon as she lay down she drifted off into sleep.

The third night she hiked further north along the river, up past the edge of Mount Hegel, up past the Backlands where the Cascade River cut into the mountains. It was the area where she had been found all those years ago, a little shivering baby Cub alone by the Great River. There was a tower there, on the rise of a hill. It had been built in the months after she had been found, and bears had kept watch there for over a year afterward. But there had never been a sighting of any other bears. No clue as to where Ember might have come from. "Somewhere up the river," was the best anyone could guess.

Ember had climbed the ladder up into the tower, looking out high above the river as she ate her sandwich, with the moonlight glistening through the spray. Somewhere out there was Heflin's Reach, a thin rocky island far out in the river. On a clear day you could see the towering pines that clung to the rocky ground in the midst of the torrent.

She had gone a little further north that night and then had turned east again, coming eventually to the Backlands and the banks of the Cascade River. And then, as the first glow of dawn could be seen in the east, she had come to the edge of the Lower Woods and to the meadow where her journey began.

That was yesterday. She had done her best to stay awake during the daylight hours, swimming and visiting all of her favorite spots. She had almost fallen asleep after lunch, lying back on the soft grass by the stream. She had started to drift off when she heard a faint rustling in the grass, and then Squiggle had come bounding out and hopped up onto her tummy. She had played with the little bunny and his mother until late in the afternoon.

As evening had come, she sat down by her campfire, thinking back on the past months and all she had seen and done in these woods.

"There is something about being out in the wild," Merridy would say. "Something that can catch up your heart and set it soaring. That's what you will find on your Adventure, Ember. Dreams and ideas that have been buried in the bustle will pop up all around you in the quiet, open spaces."

She had slept out in the open that night, curled up in her sleeping bag by the fire, the sky bright and bristling with stars. She had lain there listening to the gurgle of the stream and the soft whisper of the wind in the treetops until sleep carried her off into dreams. She had awoken that morning to warm sunlight on her face, and now she sat by her backpack tightening the straps and preparing to leave.

It was the Day of Return. The last day of her Adventure. The boy Cubs in the mountains and the girl Cubs out in the Lower Lands would all be getting ready to come home. But they would no longer be Cubs. They would all return to Haven now as Young Bears. Ember was almost bursting with excitement. In just a few hours she would see Gittel and Skye, and Calico and Laila and the rest of her girl Cub friends. They would all meet on the path at the foot of the Little Cliffs and come into Haven at noon in a joyful parade. The boy Cubs would return in the late afternoon, flying in on their gliders as they gathered at Glider Leap. Then they'd all come down together to the base of the tower, where there would be feasting and singing till late in the night. The whole of Haven would be there. And tomorrow—Ember's heart was pounding at the thought—tomorrow would be Riverbed Day!

It had been ten years since the last Riverbed Day. The village had been buzzing with excitement all year. On Riverbed Day the Cascade River would be stopped, held back by enormous dam walls as the water cisterns built in caves under the mountains were refilled. While the waters were stopped, the bears of Haven would explore the dry riverbed, searching for river gems and polished river rocks. There would be gold too, of course, in lumpy, chunky nuggets. It was useful for decorations, but it was the colored stones the bears prized the most. Everyone would be out searching until the dam was reopened at sunset, and the Cascade River would roar onward again.

Ember took one last look around the meadow and smiled at the swaying rows of daisies spelling out her name. Squiggle was sitting on the soft, short grass by the river, gazing up at her sadly as his mother nuzzled his ear. The other rabbits were there, too, with a chattering scurry of squirrels.

"Goodbye," she whispered, her voice sounding a little shaky.

She turned then, and with a last wave of farewell, went off into the trees. She hiked past the big oak and down through the ferns, stopping for a moment to look up at the little birds, still happy and chirping in their nest up in the branches. Ember wiped away a tear, surprised at how sad it felt to be leaving. It had been a wonderful summer out in the forest. Though she couldn't wait to get home again, she knew she would miss this place.

It was mid-morning when Ember finally came out of the trees, bounding up onto the path that led toward Haven.

"Ember!"

Ember could recognize Gittel's excited shout coming from way up near the foothills.

"Ember! Ember!"

Ember put her paw up to shade her eyes and saw a little shape jumping up and down in the distance.

"Gittel!" she shouted happily, taking off at a run toward her friend.

Gittel was running, too, almost toppling over as she dropped her pack in the path and threw her arms around Ember.

"Woo-hoooo!!" Gittel squealed, too excited to find the right words, and Ember squealed, too. They were both crying happily and jumping up and down together.

"I *missed* you!" Gittel gasped, trying to catch her breath. "Oh, Ember! You're a sight for sore eyes!"

"And tired eyes," Ember giggled. "What a summer!"

They sat together on the path, talking excitedly as the clouds drifted lazily by in the morning sky.

" ... and I even simmered a pinecone in honey-sauce to see what it might taste like!" Gittel was saying. "Four words, Ember: DON'T. EVEN. TRY. IT!"

Ember was crying with laughter. "That's four words!" she sniffled.

And they both burst out again in happy giggles and snorts.

Ember was wiping her eyes with her sleeve when suddenly she stopped and leapt to her feet. Gittel saw it too and was already starting to squeal.

"Skye!!" they both cried at exactly the same time, and they took off at a run down the road to meet her.

18
The Day of Return

There was a thunderous cheer as Ember and her friends came up from the Little Cliffs and onto the main street of Haven. The whole village had gathered to see the girl Cubs' return, though they were no longer girl Cubs—they were now Young Bears.

Ember grinned at Skye as the crowd broke out into one of the old Adventure songs. "The Fair Streets of Haven," it was called, and it had always made Ember smile since there was really only one street in Haven. The rest were just pathways and alleys. And there was a line in the song about "the smell of Terfuffenny Cakes." No one knew what a Terfuffenny Cake was, or what one might possibly smell like. It *was* a song about coming home though, and as the chorus rang through the village, Ember found herself singing along with all her heart.

The mayor was standing in the middle of the street, and as the song came to an end he raised his paw and the crowd went suddenly silent. The little Cubs looked up at their parents, not sure of what was going on, but even they were quiet as the mayor began to speak.

"Bears of Haven!" he said in his booming "official" voice, "Do you see Cubs?"

"No!" roared the crowd.

"Do you see Young Bears?" he shouted.

Ember giggled with excitement.

"Yes!" roared the crowd, and then everything was a riot of laughing and shouting as the bears rushed to welcome home the Adventurers. There were hugs and kisses and pats on the back as Ember and her friends were engulfed by the crowd. Little Cubs ran in all directions, scooting under grown-ups' legs and trying to get close to the new Young Bears. The littlest ones squealed and chased each other. And a few of them, who were so excited they didn't know what to do, just stood there with their arms out and spun around in circles.

Ember took it all in blissfully, her face beaming with a happy grin.

"Ember!" came a familiar voice through the noise, and Ember felt her eyes suddenly brimming with tears as she saw Merridy squeezing through the crowd toward her.

"Mama!" she gasped. Ember flung her arms around the older bear, pressing her face against her mother's cheek as Merridy hugged her tightly.

"Oh I missed you, sweet Ember," Merridy whispered, finally standing back a little to get a good look at her daughter. "You *do* look like a different bear! All grown up and big and ... "

" ... muddy!" Ember laughed, sniffling away a happy tear that was trickling down her cheek.

"Yes! Definitely in need of a hot bath!" Merridy chuckled. "Come on, I've got lunch ready for you at the library."

They squeezed through the crowd, greeting friends and family as they made their way down the street. "The bath is already run," Merridy said as they came inside. "I had a feeling that might be something you'd like to do first. Take your time and then we'll have a long talk over lunch."

<hr/>

"So you crept right by the cottage and we didn't even notice!" Merridy was saying as they sat in the library. "I wondered if you might spend a night down there on your hike, but I didn't hear a thing!"

Ember grinned. "I was hoping you and Fergal and Mika might be there. Just to get a chance to see you. It was a little close though. It was all I could do not to run up and give you hugs. Especially when I saw you ..." Ember's voice trailed off.

" ... when you saw us remembering C.J.," Merridy said kindly. She reached over and gave Ember's paw a squeeze. "We do that every time we're together down by The Precipice," she said. "We get up early and watch the sunrise, and we think of our friend. He is special to them, too, not just to me." Merridy smiled. "C.J. and Fergal were friends from the time they were little Cubs. Bears would say they explored the whole of Haven before they could even walk. And as young Cubs we all explored the Lower Lands. It was C.J. and Fergal who discovered the ruins in the hidden valley, and they both drew the plans to restore the cottage. When C.J. went over The Precipice ..." Merridy's voice trailed off and a tear rolled down her cheek. She was quiet for a long moment, looking out the tall library windows.

"Oh I miss him, Ember," she said softly.

"How can you stand it, Mama?" Ember whispered. "Not knowing where he is—waiting for him all this time?"

Merridy smiled, a soft, sure smile that was solid and deep.

"He's a bear worth waiting for," she said, putting her arm around Ember's shoulder. They stood quietly for a long time, looking out toward The Precipice.

It was late afternoon when they came out onto the main street, joining the noisy procession on its way to the Lookout. Bears cheered when they saw Ember, and little Merritt came running over to walk beside her, holding paws. The street was filled with sounds of laughter and shouting, and Ember breathed deeply, taking in the delicious smell of fresh pies and hot bread. She could already see the long tables at the foot of the Lookout, piled high with mountains of food.

"I hope you're hungry!" Merridy chuckled, nodding in the direction of the feast. "We better get there before Growly and Ash though! You know how they can eat!"

Ember laughed, looking up into the sky to see if there was any sign of gliders yet. The boy Cubs would be flying in soon, each one circling above Glider Leap till it was his turn to land. Then they would all come down the mountain together, to the cheers of all the village.

"See anything yet?" Merridy asked. She put her paw up to shade her eyes and gazed into the distance.

"Glider ho!" There was a sudden cry from the crowd. As Ember looked up she could see a flag waving from the balcony of the Lookout. Everyone rushed forward, calling excitedly as they raced to the tower.

"There it is!" someone called, pointing off toward a tiny shape swinging out around the cliffs of Janika Mountain, just across the valley.

"There's another!" someone cried, pointing excitedly to the east.

There was a shout from the tower, "Three now ... four! Two more coming around."

Soon the sky above the Backlands was filled with tiny specks, racing past the soaring cliffs, up toward the Leap.

"Eleven!" came the cry. "Two more coming round!" Then, "Fourteen!"

Ember was almost bursting with excitement.

The gliders were beginning to land up on Glider Leap, swirling down onto the platform as others swooped in over the valley.

Ember turned back toward the east, straining to see if the final glider had appeared yet.

"Come on, Fifteen!" Ember whispered, starting to feel a little concerned. The fourteenth glider was already well across the Backlands.

A hush was beginning to fall over the gathered crowd, leaving just the sound of a few nervous whispers. There was no sign from the Lookout. Where was the last glider?

Minutes passed, and then more minutes, as bears looked at each other with worried expressions and then back toward the sky. The fourteenth glider had landed now.

Fergal was up on the tall rock with the mayor, talking earnestly and pointing out toward the east. The mayor was nodding, and suddenly Fergal started to run up the pathway that led to Glider Leap.

"Look!" someone cried. High up on the pathway another bear was racing down the mountain, leaping and stumbling as he hurried toward Haven.

The minutes dragged by, feeling like hours to Ember as she nervously waited.

"Here they come," someone shouted, pointing toward the shapes of Fergal and one of the Young Bears hurrying together toward the Lookout.

"Ash!" Ember gasped, recognizing her friend's orange and green flight jacket.

She looked up at Merridy with panic in her eyes.

Merridy took Ember's paw and squeezed it tightly, trying to smile. Her face looked strained and worried though, and there were tears in the corners of her eyes.

"Growly!" Ember cried. She didn't have to wait for Ash's news. And as Ember saw the look on Merridy's face, it was clear she felt it, too.

19
Missing

mber's eyes were blurry with tears as she raced up the path, running with all her strength toward Glider Leap. Growly! Merridy was close behind her, and she could see Farren and Growly's mother, Edolie, far up ahead, with Ash running beside them. There were others coming up the mountain, too, members of the Rescue Committee and many of the Cubs and Young Bears who were skilled at flying.

Ember wiped her eyes as she ran, her ears filled with the sound of her pounding heart and her panting and sniffles. Growly! How could he be missing?

Merridy had told her of the first time she and Growly had met. "You could barely even crawl; you'd only been with me a few days. I sat you on the rug at Growly's place, and when he saw you he squealed with delight and waved his little arms in the air. He waved so hard he fell right over, and then he cried because he was stuck." Ember had giggled.

"Well, Edolie picked him up and carried him over to you. When she put him down on the rug he threw his little arms around you and you both toppled over, giggling."

Now, as Ember raced up the mountain, memories flooded into her mind. The first thing she could remember of Growly was sitting next to him in the sandpit as a warm, summer breeze ruffled the fur around her ears. Growly had put a paw-full of sand right on his head, and he had chuckled like it was the best joke ever. They were both still crawling at that time. She could remember scooting around with him on the floor of the library while Merridy dusted the rows of books. And there were birthdays and picnics and reading times and feasts. So many wonderful memories. How could he be missing?

"We'll find him, Ember."

Ember blinked and glanced over to see Skye coming up next to her on the path. She had her flight cap tied tight and was buttoning up her flight coat as she ran. Ember couldn't say anything. She felt too close to tears, but she nodded gratefully to her friend, and they both ran harder as they came to the stairs below Glider Leap.

Gliders were already beginning to launch, one after another while bears shouted from the landing platform. As the pilots lifted off, they circled up into the sky, flying in a tight formation and then zooming out over the Backlands toward the mountain valleys. Farren had given the orders as soon as he arrived on the platform: two gliders for each valley, search on the ground through the night, signal if help is needed. Many of the Young Bears were ready to go, having waited up on the Leap while Ash went to find Farren. Ember hurried up the steps, her long dress wrapping around her legs in the strong, mountain breeze. She had worn it especially for the boy Cubs' return—for Growly's homecoming. She sniffed back a tear and wiped her eyes with her long sleeve. As she reached the top of the stairs, she hurried through the wide doorway into the storage room of Glider Leap. Many of the storage racks were empty, with pilots already up on the roof or in the air. Ember hurried over to her rack and pulled out a jacket and flight pants from her locker.

"I'll get your glider ready," came a voice from behind her. Ember knew who it was right away.

"Oh Gittel, thank you!" Tears were streaming down Ember's face. "I'm sorry, I'm ..."

Gittel threw her arms around her friend and hugged her tightly. "The whole village is heading out, Ember. We'll find him."

Ember sniffled and nodded, looking up at her friend with red-rimmed eyes.

"The changing room is empty. Just get dressed, and I'll have your glider ready for you in no time," Gittel said with an encouraging smile.

Ember hurried into a small room off to the right of the glider storage. It had a bed in the corner and a couple of coat racks. Nothing fancy, just a place to rest if you had to spend the night at Glider Leap. Ember closed the door behind her and dressed quickly, buttoning her jacket as she headed up the stairs toward the landing platform. She could hear shouts and calls and Farren's voice as he gave instructions to the bears.

"If there's no sign of him in the valley you're assigned to, get some sleep and wait for me to fly in at first light. If Edolie and I don't find him tonight, we'll have plans ready for searching in the mountains tomorrow."

There was shout as another glider took off.

"Ember!" Ember recognized Edolie's voice calling her as she came out onto the platform. Growly's mother looked tired and strained, but she managed a smile as she hurried over.

"Edolie!" Ember sobbed, her voice sounding croaky.

"We'll find him, dear," Edolie said kindly. "Farren and I are about to leave for his valley. He's probably just having trouble with his glider. If he had been hurt, the bees would have let us know." Her voice sounded a little unsure, however. "We would like you and Merridy to go to the Honey Well though, just to check. Merridy knows

Bee better than anyone, and maybe we missed something, and ..." Edolie looked like she was about to cry. She took a deep breath and then smiled again shakily. "Search the Belden Valley with Merridy when you're done. You'll both have to sleep there."

Ember nodded, and Edolie turned and hurried back to her husband. He was tightening the straps on his glider with the help of two young Cubs.

In a few minutes both Farren and Edolie were ready, standing on the platform with their gliders. "Everyone not flying, meet the mayor at the Lookout. He will be leading the search of the Lower Lands. Search well!" Farren called. Then he was off at a run down the platform, leaping out into the late afternoon sky. Edolie was right behind him, and the two of them circled upward for a moment before racing off eastward toward Janika Mountain and the valleys beyond.

"Ready?" Merridy asked. She was hitched up to her glider and looked over at Ember with a tired smile.

Ember nodded, pulling down her flight goggles.

Skye was almost ready with her glider. She would be searching one of the far valleys with two of the girls. Her encouraging smile stuck with Ember as she took off down the platform and leapt into the air.

The sky above the Backland Valley was full of gliders, racing out into the mountains that stretched toward the east. There would not be much time to search before sunset. The sky was already changing color in the late afternoon light. Just enough time to reach the valleys and get started. But at least they could keep searching on the ground. Flying in the dark was far too dangerous, but Ember knew every pilot would search the valleys with lamps late into the night.

Ember raced over the Backland Valley, gazing down for a moment at the tall cliffs and steep, rocky banks that ran on either side of the Cascade River. Far up ahead she could see the enormous river gates, where the Building Committee would be making checks and preparations for Riverbed Day. They had been up there for days, and already the old water wheels would be beginning to turn, slowly pushing the river gates closed so the cisterns could be refilled.

Ember couldn't think about Riverbed Day now though. Pushing the nose of her glider down a little, she dove until she caught a stronger air current, rising up with a whoosh as Janika Mountain loomed in front of her. She swung to the left, glancing around to see Merridy right behind. The jagged cliffs of the mountain rushed by in a blur to her right, the familiar shape of Honey Guard rock rising high up above. Just a little farther ...

Pushing hard to the right, Ember came swooping around the far side of the mountain, soaring out over Belden Valley with its carpet of wildflowers and sparkling lake. The last rays of sunlight were glistening on the smooth water, sending flickers of light across the valley as dusk settled in. Ember turned hard again, swooping up toward a platform on the side of the cliffs. The platform disappeared into a tall, gaping cavern—the Honey Well of Hegel, the home of the bees.

20
The Home of the Bees

Ember skidded to a halt, quickly unfastening her harness and hauling her glider to the side of the platform. Merridy circled over the valley above the cliffs, coming back around a few times until she saw Ember had her glider secure and was safely out of the way. With a final turn out over the lake, she came swooping in toward the platform, pulling up at the last moment and coming to a wobbling stop on the smooth stone.

"It's almost night, Mama," Ember said as she helped Merridy with her harness.

Merridy looked over toward the cavern with a frown. "It is," she sighed, "but perhaps they are still active. I haven't been here this late in the day. Oh, I hope they can help us."

Ember could feel tears coming again. It seemed they were always lurking there, just waiting for her to think of Growly. She took a deep breath and tried to hold them back. There would be time for tears later if ...

No! Ember pushed the thought from her mind. They *would* find Growly … somehow.

Merridy could see the troubled look in her daughter's eyes. "Come on," she said, putting her arm over Ember's shoulder. "If he's hurt, the bees will let us know—and if he's not hurt, then we just have to find him. He may have even been found already."

With their gliders secured, they hurried back across the platform, stopping at the mouth of the cave to light one of the lanterns stored just inside. Ember took a last glance out over the Belden Valley, buried in long shadows and the last crimson glow of sunset. The tall, dark shapes of the mountains rose beyond the lake, soaring jagged peaks and plunging cliffs that fell into the other mountain valleys along the line of the Alps. Growly *was* out there somewhere. He must be.

"Ready?" Merridy asked, holding up the lantern and giving Ember an encouraging smile.

Ember nodded, looking up at her mother's face bathed in the warm flickering glow of the lantern. There was always something about that face that made her feel safe, that made even the hardest day feel a little brighter.

"Ready," she whispered, and with the lamp held in front of them, they made their way into the cavern.

The Honey Well cave had been there long before the days of Hegel, though he had drawn the plans for the platform and helped seed the valley with the bears of his time. It had just been a mountain cave when he found it, but he had seen that the Belden Valley would be a wonderful place for the bees, and the cave a safe home to build their honeycombs and hives. That was long, long ago, back before there were any buildings in Haven. A time wrapped up in the legends of countless library books. *"Hegel dug the cave himself..."* one story went, *"and the bees carried off the pebbles all the way to The Precipice."*

"And when Hegel was done, a giant bee carried him off over the Alps to find his long lost love, Janika," Growly would joke, though Ember got the feeling he almost wished it were true. "Wouldn't that have been a wonderful ending to Hegel's story?"

It would have been a nice ending (though Ember wasn't sure about the giant bee part). The truth was no one knew what became of Hegel. He walked off into the mountains and was never seen again.

Bears had been coming to the Honey Well since those ancient times, flying in from Glider Leap to collect honey. The bears of Haven were free to take as much as they needed. That's the way it had always been, since Hegel and his friends helped the bees by seeding the valley. The bears made sure the fields were filled with wildflowers, and the bees watched for danger and gave warning to the bears. It was a friendship of sorts that had lasted through the ages, and every Cub had to learn a little of the language of the bees.

"They don't speak like we do," Merridy would tell a class of little Cubs. "They dance and they wiggle. It all means different things. Hegel was the first one to figure it out, and no, he didn't learn it from a giant talking bee like it says in *The Eastward Chronicles*! He learned it from just staring for hours and hours at the bees in their hives, noticing their patterns and then figuring out what they meant. It took him a long time to learn much at all—years to learn just a handful of words. But he kept at it, and he learned, and it saved his whole village. It was the warning of the bees that brought them all the way to the mountains. And that is why you must all learn at least one word in Bee. Every bear should know the Bee word for danger."

Merridy knew their language better than any bear in Haven. "I learned a lot from books," she would say with a smile. That always made Growly's grandparents laugh.

"Really!" Fergal would laugh, raising an eyebrow. "Books, you say?"

Merridy would blush. "Well, C.J. *might* have had a little to do with it."

Now as they walked into the tall cavern, Ember could see the shelves of pots along the walls and the ancient carvings in the stone. And further back in the shadows she could hear a growing hum of the bees in their hives around the Honey Well.

Merridy turned to Ember with a grin. It was not too late in the evening. The bees were still active. She hurried across the open floor toward the well, slowing down as she came closer.

"Here is close enough," she whispered, placing the lantern on the floor and motioning for Ember to kneel down beside her. "They know we're here," Merridy said excitedly. "Can you hear the difference in the hum?"

Ember nodded. "Here they come."

There was a sound of buzzing nearby, and soon the floor around the lantern was filled with bees, moving and dancing in a tangle of circles and turns. Merridy gazed down at the bees for a long time, watching the movements carefully as the minutes ticked by. Ember could see the concentration on her mother's face as she leaned in close, her eyes following the tiny insects as they moved about on the cool, stone floor. Ember recognized a few words, but nothing that looked anything like danger.

"Anything, Mama?" Ember whispered, peering over at Merridy.

Merridy looked up and sighed, shaking her head seriously, her face still crinkled in concentration.

"The weather and Cub flight. The kind of things you would expect. But nothing of injury or danger of any kind. If Growly were hurt they would be certain to know."

"Oh, Mama!" Ember sighed. "He must be alright then!"

Merridy nodded, her face slowly brightening into a smile.

"He must have had problems with his glider. Farren and Edolie are probably with him right now, sitting drinking tea while they wait for the morning."

The bees were beginning to fly back toward their hives now, circling above the bears' heads for a moment in farewell before buzzing off into the darkness.

"Let's go down to the valley," Merridy said as she got to her feet. "We'll have to take it carefully. Looks like it's already dark outside."

They made their way out onto the platform again, standing for a moment in the cool, evening breeze as they gazed out toward the mountains.

"Look!" Ember gasped, pointing out into the night toward a dim speck of light far in the distance.

"It could be Ash. He was supposed to be in the second valley."

"There will be lights out wandering all through the mountains tonight, at least for the next few hours."

They made their way across the platform and onto a wide pathway that cut down the side of the cliff. In places there were steep stairs, smooth and worn with the years, and roped walkways reaching out over the heights. Slowly they made their way downward until finally Ember felt the soft spring of grass under her feet, and she ran out into the valley.

"Let's search the west side first," Merridy said, as she came down onto the grass. "We should be able to cover the whole valley before midnight.

They searched till late into the evening, looking carefully behind every rock and bush for any sign of Growly. There was no reason he would be here. His valley was miles away. Still, if there were any chance he was in the Belden, they had to look.

As the moon rose high above them, they finally came to the end of their search, snuggling tiredly into their sleeping bags with the stars spread out glistening above them. Ember stared up at the night sky for a long time, thinking of Growly until she finally drifted off into sleep. The sound of shouts awakened her, as the first rays of sunlight came up above The Precipice.

21
Farren's Report

Ember sat up with a start, looking around blearily in the direction the shouts were coming from. Merridy was already on her feet, gazing up into the sky as a dark shape whooshed by overhead.

"Ember! Merridy!" came a cry from above. It was Skye. Ember recognized her voice right away.

The dark shape was only over them for a moment, and then it was racing out over the meadow and turning to come back around. In the dim morning light, Ember could see the familiar patterns on the wing of her friend's glider: swirling clouds with a large eagle in the middle. That was Skye's favorite kind of bird.

As Skye swooped in closer, Ember saw a small bundle drop from the glider.

"A message!" Skye called. "See you at the Leap!"

Merridy waved her arm as Skye whooshed by, and Ember called out to let her know she had seen the bundle. The glider turned hard to the right and in a moment caught an updraft near the cliffs. Skye soared upward and out toward the back of the valley, and in a few moments she was gone.

"Just over here!" Merridy called, hurrying to where the bundle had dropped in the grass. It was a rolled up piece of paper, tied with string and weighted with a small rock.

"It's from Farren," Merridy said earnestly, holding the paper close to her face as she tried to read in the dim light. "We're to meet at Glider Leap." She looked at Ember with a serious face. "There's no sign of Growly yet, Ember. We're going to have to widen the search."

Ember felt her heart sink and a cold shiver run down her back. Growly!

"Get your things quickly, dear," Merridy said softly, noticing the hopeless look settling on Ember's face. "Growly is out there. He needs us, Ember. He needs you." Merridy touched Ember's face gently with her paw, looking intently into her daughter's eyes. "Have hope my sweet, brave daughter. Don't give up on him."

Ember noticed a feeling rising up inside that almost took her by surprise. And though worry and panic were still swirling around her, the hint of a smile crept onto her face.

"I ... I couldn't, Mama," Ember felt her heart thumping as she realized. "I could *never* give up on him.

Oh ... *Mama!*" Ember threw her arms around Merridy. "Now I really understand. I could *never* give up!"

"A bear worth waiting for," Merridy whispered. There were tears trickling down her cheeks.

<hr />

They raced across the valley, fastening their packs as they ran through the early morning shadows. Ember's heart was pounding with fear and hope and a new determination that was growing by the moment. Beams of bright morning light were stretching out over the mountains, bathing the pathway up the cliff face in orange and red. Merridy and Ember hurried along the stony trail, leaping up the twisting stairs and across the hanging bridges, until they finally reached the platform at the front of the Honey Well.

"You first," Merridy panted, helping Ember into her glider harness and checking the straps. "Don't wait for me," she said with a smile. "I'll be right behind you."

Ember pounded down the platform and leapt into the air, feeling the wind lift her glider high out over the Belden Valley. The gently rippling waters of the lake glistened as the sunrise streamed into the valley. She raced on northward, looking down on the rolling stretches of wildflowers until the ground began to rise sharply and she saw the rocky cliffs of the Backland Valley. Making a wide, arching turn to the left, she came swooping around the back of Janika Mountain, the jagged shape of Honey Guard rock looming up through the shadows as she raced by.

Haven and Mount Hegel were still bathed in night. The piercing beams of morning light had not reached there yet, though the main street was filled with bears and the windows were lit. Ember could see tiny dots of lamplight moving out toward the Lookout and others heading down toward the pathway to the Lower Lands.

There were lights on Glider Leap, too. Ember could see shadows moving up on the rooftop and the waving glow of signal lamps on the landing platform. She glanced back at the dim shadow of Merridy's glider coming around Janika Mountain, small and distant behind her. As she came closer, Ember could see Skye was waving the signal light. She stood out on the platform swinging a large lamp in one paw and signaling with her other. There were gliders out on the rooftop. Three or four with bears gathered all around. Light streamed out of the windows below, and Ember could see the shadows of movement inside the main room of Glider Leap.

She swooped in toward the platform, feeling the solid thud as her boots touched the stone and she came stumbling to a stop. Skye hurried over, helping her quickly unfasten and move her glider to the side so Merridy could land.

"Farren is downstairs," she gasped, taking Ember by the paw and pulling her toward the stairs. "He wanted to see you as soon as you arrived. Come on!"

They hurried down the stairway and burst into the storage room, where a large group of bears was gathered around a long table. Farren was at the end, and he looked up suddenly as he heard Skye and Ember enter.

"Ember," he said seriously as the room went suddenly quiet. "I ... I'm sorry. We haven't been able to find him." Farren's face looked tired and there was a heaviness in his voice. "Edolie is out with Ash and the others. They will search the mountain valleys again in the morning light. I'm afraid though, that we will need to widen our search. No one has seen any sign of Growly yet."

Ember nodded, and Skye put her arm around her friend's shoulder.

"All of the building crew is out at the Cascade River. They have to go ahead with filling the cisterns. But the rest of the village is heading out to search. It will just be the baby Cubs and their mothers at Riverbed Day this time."

Riverbed Day! Ember had completely forgotten. It was to be the biggest celebration in years. Now all anyone could think of was finding Growly.

"I'll be asking Merridy to search from the air around Haven," Farren continued. "I need you two to take the region on the other side of the Cascade, all the way up to the Great River where it comes out in the north."

Ember and Skye gasped.

"I know it's a wide area," Farren said softly. "We'll send others out once they come in from searching the valleys. But ... " Farren's voice fell quiet for a moment, and he took a deep breath before he continued, "he could be anywhere. We have to look everywhere we can, even out over the Banks. If you see him, try to land and signal. We'll have spotters up here on the Leap."

Ember nodded, and Skye suddenly smiled as the door swung open.

"Gittel!" Ember cried, as her friend and three Young Bears burst into the room. She was dressed in a flight coat and pants, and she held a small telescope in one paw. When she saw Ember, her eyes filled with tears and she ran over and threw her arms around Ember in a tight hug.

"He's all right!" she whispered. "I just *know* it!"

Ember nodded, a gentle smile spreading across her face. "Let's find him then," she said. "My glider is ready on the roof."

The sun was peeking around Janika Mountain when they came back out onto the platform. The main street of Haven was still busy with bears, tiny specks running this way and that in the village far below. Ember hardly noticed. In her mind she was going over the directions Farren had shown her on the map.

"East along the Backland Valley, along the flow of the Cascade, and then north when it turns. Skye will take the western side and come back eastward past the next mountains. Both of you head out to the Banks after that." Farren had spoken quickly and seriously as he explained the directions, but when he finished he gave Ember and Skye a kind smile. "Be careful, you two," he said, ruffling the fur around Ember's ear with his paw and patting Skye on her shoulder. "Don't fly too close to the Great River. You know how bad the winds are there."

Ember watched now as Skye ran down the platform and leapt into the air, her glider caught in sunlight as she rose up above the Leap.

"Ready?" Gittel whispered with an encouraging nod.

"Ready," Ember answered, though that was not at all the way she felt.

22
Goldentail

The morning sunlight was reaching down into the Backland Valley, lighting the cliffs and rocky slopes scattered with trees, all the way down to the banks of the Cascade River. Ember swooped downward, feeling the wind whistle past her face as she raced along to the east. She was stunned at the sight of the dry riverbed below. Just yesterday it had been a thundering, rushing torrent, pounding through the Backlands on its way to The Precipice. She had never seen the Cascade stopped like this.

The sunlight glistened on gemstones, sparkling on pools of water nestled in the rocks. The riverbed was deep; she could see it now that the water was gone. How wonderful it would be to wander along it and search for gems. Not today though.

Ember pulled the nose of her glider a little higher, catching an updraft as she turned to the left, following the curve of the riverbed as it cut its way northward. Just a little further and ...

Ember gasped. The riverbed narrowed, walled in by towering cliffs. And there, just a short distance ahead were the River Gates—tall wooden walls braced with beams of solid iron. She had never seen them working. For as long as she had been in Haven they had just been sunken in the cliffs, waiting for Riverbed Year when the giant cogs and water wheels would heave them into place. Once every ten years. That was enough to fill the underground cisterns, built in the maze of caves and caverns that ran underneath the mountains.

There were bears up on the gates, peering down into the dry riverbed and checking the bracings and joints. It was the Building Committee. They were in charge of the maintenance of the gates and of all the designs and devices that helped the village in the heights. They had been up here all week, working and testing and fixing anything that needed to be replaced. Ember pulled the nose of her glider up, soaring higher as she sped toward the gates. There was a cheer from the bears on the wall, and Ember gave a quick wave. There was Ruslan, waving his gloves and hammer, and Pepper, dressed in her brightest overalls and cap. Other bears were running out of the caverns in the cliffs, curious to see what the cheering was about.

Ember soared up past them, clearing the top of the gates and coming out over an amazing sight. The river spread into an enormous lake between the mountains, pouring into caves that had once been high on the slopes of the Cascade. There was a rumbling sound mixing with the whistle of the wind as Ember swooped out over the newly forming lake. The mountains now towered all around her. It was the edge of the Alps, and this was the farthest the bears ever went. Up ahead the peaks rose high into the clouds, their cliffs coated in ice and whipped by mountain winds. Even in the summer it was freezing up there.

Ember turned her glider to the left, heading toward a narrow valley between the peaks that led westward to the Great River. Skye would be somewhere up ahead, beginning her search for Growly in the northern part of the Banks.

As she came in between the cliffs, Ember scanned the valley floor for any sign of Growly. She couldn't think of any reason he would be up this far, but still they must look. The ground was rocky, dotted with small groves of pine. A stream cut through the middle of the valley, twisting through the boulders on its way toward the Cascade. Ember had spent a night up here once, camping with the other Cubs her age the summer before last. Many of the older bears had come, too. It was a sort of summer tradition—Night Amongst the Peaks it was called. Mika joked it really should be called Shiver Amongst the Peaks. They had wakened to find snow on the ground and their breakfast sandwiches frozen. Hot chocolate had never felt so good as it did that morning.

There was no sign of anyone below. All was still and quiet, draped in the shadows of the early morning. Ember swooped back and forth along the valley, staying as low as she could as she made her way to the west. At times she doubled back to make sure she hadn't missed anything. There were many caves and rocky places where a bear could find some shelter. When she came to trees she would circle overhead, watching for smoke or any sign of movement. She saw a rabbit or two and the flutter of birds in the branches. She even saw a large fish leaping in the stream. But there was no sign of Growly.

By mid-morning she had come to the end of the valley. It had taken a long time. Every half hour she had to soar up into the heights to show Gittel and the other spotters on Glider Leap that she was OK. It made the searching slower but it was very important. Flying in the valleys could be dangerous, and the spotters were there to send help if needed.

The sun was getting high in the sky when Ember soared around a rocky cliff and came out above the hills and open lands called the Banks. Sunlight was suddenly all around her, and Ember had to blink until her eyes adjusted to the light. There were eagles out toward the Great River, circling high above the hills that ran along the shore. The air there was full of mist and spray, with only a faint glimpse of green in far in the distance. The eagles turned and jostled in the wind, buffeted by the gusts that blew up from The Precipice. Flying near the Great River was always dangerous. The winds there were always rough.

Ember peered out over the Banks, looking for any sign of Skye. She should be out there somewhere.

Something suddenly rushed past her on the left, swooping down below for a moment and then soaring out in front.

"Goldentail?" Ember gasped.

The eagle turned and then flew up beside her, speeding along next to the glider and calling with a screeching cry. Goldentail looked at her for a moment, and it almost seemed as if he nodded before swooping out in front again and turning back around.

Ember stared at the enormous eagle in astonishment. She had never seen him act like this before. "What are you up to?" she whispered, trying to guess what he might do next.

"Emmm-berrrr!"

There was another flash of something off to her right, and Ember turned to see Skye swooping up next to her.

"Skye!" she shouted above the flapping of the gliders and the whistle of the wind. "You just about scared me out of the air!"

Skye's face looked alarmed. "Across the river, Ember! I saw it!"

Ember was about to ask her what she had seen, when Goldentail suddenly swooped out in front of them, shrieking out a cry and tilting his wings back and forth. It was a flying signal. Every Cub knew it.

"He did the signal!" Skye cried in astonishment. "Ember! Did you *see* that?"

Ember nodded, hardly believing her eyes. "He wants us to follow!" she shouted. Goldentail must have learned the signal from watching the gliders over the years.

The eagle swooped back around and came up between Skye and Ember, screeching to them both and then soaring off to the right.

"Back toward the mountains?" Skye shouted. Goldentail was racing off toward the Alps.

Ember was silent for a moment, her mind racing with questions. What if they'd just imagined the signal. What about Growly?

Goldentail circled back toward the gliders, letting out another cry before turning again toward the mountains.

"We have to see!" Ember shouted. "He's never done *this* before. Something isn't right." Ember's heart was pounding. What if he's found Growly?

Skye nodded and banked off in Goldentail's direction, and Ember pulled hard on the bar of her glider. The wing tipped down and she began to circle around after Skye, the both of them now headed directly for the mountains.

23
The Danger in the Peaks

Goldentail flew into the valley between the peaks, soaring down over the twisting stream and then zooming upward on the wind. Skye was not far behind him, and Ember pushed her glider faster as she followed. The cliffs rushed by, stretching up into the heights on either side of the valley. Skimming Pond, the three big boulders, Tall Pine Grove. Ember counted off the landmarks as she raced along. Just a little further around this bend ...

The wings of Ember's glider flapped and hummed in the strong updraft as she raced. Patches of ice could now be seen on the cliffs. Higher and higher she went, the cliffs giving way to the snowy slopes of Flarian's Pass. It was a lower place between the peaks, a place that could be seen from Glider Leap. Ember soared higher into the sky, doing a couple of sharp turns in the air before she pushed the nose of her glider downward again. Gittel would have seen her, or one of the spotters.

Goldentail and Skye were far down the valley now, racing along between the cliffs far the distance. Ember cut down over Flarian's Pass, flying over the snowy slopes as she tried to catch up. At the end of the pass were more cliffs, and Ember tilted her wing to the left, dipping back down into the valley. As she came lower, she could see the rush of rocks and trees speeding by in a blur below her. Fishleap Rapids ... the Blackwall Canyon. Around this corner comes the Long Stretch. Ember swooped around the curve and saw Skye and Goldentail.

They sped onward through the valley for a long time, racing past the familiar places she had hiked through in the past. She had flown this way many times, too. It was part of a Cub's training. One more turn, just up ahead.

They shot around the curve and came out above the Cascade River. It was the place where the river was banking up into a lake—a wide, open place that was usually green and grassy. Water now covered the whole area, smooth and calm down toward the River Gates, but churning and frothing to the east where the Cascade thundered out of the Alps.

Goldentail raced across the water, toward the eastern side where the air was thick with spray. There was a canyon over there. It stretched for a mile or so eastward before ending in icy cliffs at the place where the Cascade River came out from under the mountains. The valley was a wild place, full of jagged chunks of rock and ragged groves of pine. Biting wind whistled down from the cliffs there, even in the middle of summer, and the spray from the torrent clung in icy frost on the rocks and branches of the trees.

With Goldentail in the lead, they sped into the canyon, turning hard around a long bend with the river roaring underneath. As they came around the bend, Ember let out a cry. An avalanche! The left side of the canyon was filled with snow and chunks of ice that had slammed down from the mountains, taking out a wide stretch of trees. Water from the river thundered over an enormous tangle of pines, shooting high into the air as the ice piled up amongst the trunks and branches. Ember's mind raced as she realized the danger. If the tangled dam of trees and ice broke loose, the River Gates could be smashed.

Goldentail turned and soared up above the water, circling back quickly to make sure the bears had seen.

Skye turned to follow the eagle. As she raced by, Ember could see the look of alarm on her friend's face. They had to warn the bears working at the River Gates. Ember turned her glider hard, pulling around to follow Skye and Goldentail. The eagle was circling one more time, letting out a cry that was almost lost in the roar of the river.

"Ember!!"

Ember barely heard Skye's cry as a sudden, thundering roar rose up around her.

"Emmmberrrr!!"

She looked up to see a wall of ice and snow roaring over the cliffs and down into the canyon. Ember pushed the nose of her glider downward, picking up speed. Skye shot out in front of her, turning hard into the curve of the canyon after Goldentail. The sound was almost deafening behind her, and Ember glanced back for a moment to see a thunderous roar of ice and snow pounding down into the canyon. Just a little further. There was a sudden push of wind and Ember felt herself lifted and flung forward in an icy blast, speeding toward Skye and Goldentail as she fought to gain control.

Ember wrenched on the steering bar, struggling with all her might as the force of the wind hurled her forward.

"Skye! Look out!"

Skye was right in front of her, turning in alarm as Ember hurtled toward her.

"Skye!" Ember pushed and turned her glider to the left suddenly. It was too late though. There was a loud crack and a sickening, tearing sound as the edge of Skye's glider ripped through Ember's wing.

"Ember!" Skye cried, as she watched her friend desperately try to gain control of her damaged glider. She could only watch for a moment. The force of the wind suddenly hit her and she too felt her glider lift and turn as she was thrust out of the canyon and over the lake between the mountains.

Ember was getting lower. Skye could see her struggling for lift as they whooshed out over the water. "Ember!" she cried. There was nothing she could do.

The gust of the wind suddenly fell away behind her, and Skye turned for a moment to see a frosty, dusty cloud rising up above the canyon. Her glider was damaged, too. She could feel it shake and groan, and as she looked out toward the end of her wing, she could see a wide tear. She didn't have long.

Pulling back with all her might, Skye lifted the nose of her glider into the wind, shooting up above the lake as steeply as she dared. Higher and higher she went, her glider groaning and creaking with the strain. There was Mount Hegel, far in the distance. "Oh please, Gittel," she whispered. "Someone please be looking this way."

Skye put her glider into a sharp turn, tilting the wing three times in the signal for emergency. "One more time," she gasped, turning her glider around and tilting the wing again.

Suddenly, there was a loud, ripping sound, and Skye saw the tear stretch out along the wing. In a panic she pushed the nose of her glider downward, dropping back toward the lake as the glider jostled and shook. "Come on!" she gasped, watching the lake get closer and closer. Wind whistled past her ears, joining with the pounding of her heartbeat and the wild flapping of her damaged glider.

She was almost at the water when she pulled back on the steering bar. "Come on!" she cried.

The glider swooped down over the lake, shaking and groaning as the main beam began to break. Skye looked around franticly for Ember, but there was no sign of her friend. Just mountains and water and the whistling of the wind. There was another horrible tearing sound, and Skye felt herself starting to fall. With a thudding tumble and splash, she went down into the water.

24
The Help of Friends

Ember came to the surface spluttering and coughing, splashing in the icy water with the weight of her pack. It had all happened so quickly. She had seen Skye shooting upward and Goldentail turning above the lake. The next thing she knew, she had crashed and all had been water and bubbles.

She had freed herself from her harness right away. Every Cub was trained to do that. And she had managed to get out from under the tangled mess of her glider, splashing away from the wreckage as she started to go under again. Struggling to the surface, Ember had caught a glimpse of Skye, speeding down toward the lake with her glider ripped and failing. She had gone under again and come up struggling and gasping for breath, fumbling with the straps of her backpack until it finally came free.

"Ember!" Skye's voice echoed out to her from across the water.

Ember splashed around, looking for her friend amongst the waves. There was no sign of her at first, but then she saw a shadow over her head and heard Goldentail cry out as he circled just off to her left. There was Skye, waving her arm weakly as the tip of her glider wing slipped below the surface. With a kick of her feet, Ember started off across the water, swimming with all her might. Skye was in trouble. She was flailing about, trying to keep her head above the water.

"My pack!" Skye gasped as Ember got closer. "I can't get it loose!"

Ember tugged at the straps but she couldn't loosen it either. Her paws were beginning to feel numb from the cold, mountain water.

"It's OK," Ember gasped. Her teeth were beginning to chatter. "I can drag you." She looked around frantically. They were still a long way from the shore. "Over there!" she cried. There was a sloping outcrop of rock halfway to the shore. "Be still now, Skye! I've got you."

Ember wrapped one arm around her friend and then began to swim along with the other—short, desperate strokes as they made their way slowly toward the rock. Skye kicked with her feet, trying her best to help, but she was still weak and dizzy from the crash.

Almost there. Ember could feel her whole body aching, and her teeth chattered loudly from the cold. Just a little further. With a heave she pushed Skye up onto the slope of the rock, dragging herself up as well and collapsing in an exhausted heap on the cold stone.

They both lay there for a long time, panting and gasping for breath as the water swirled past. It was getting higher quickly. Ember looked down and saw it was already rising past her boots.

"We've got to keep moving," she groaned.

Skye looked up at her in exhaustion. "Yes," she whispered. Her teeth were chattering, and she looked as though she hardly had the strength to even lift her head.

"Do you think you can make it?" Ember asked. Her croaky whisper was full of concern.

Skye managed a weak smile. "Could you bring me a glass of lemonade first? I'm enjoying the sunbathing!"

Ember grinned and pushed herself up, looking toward the rocks out across the water. The current was getting stronger. "They must have opened another cistern," Ember gasped. Look how the water is moving!"

Skye sat up with a groan and stared out at the swirling water. She didn't say anything, but she was clearly worried. "We've got to try," she whispered. "We've got to warn them."

"Hey!" There was a sudden shout from above and a shadow swept past the rock.

Ember gasped in shock and Skye just blinked in complete astonishment.

"Gittel?" she stammered, her eyes wide.

A glider swooped out over the water and turned sharply toward the shore, wobbling and coming to a stumbling crash among the grass and rocks. Goldentail, who had been circling overhead, let out a worried call.

"Yes, it's Gittel!" Ember said with a smile.

Gittel usually did her best to stay away from gliders, and her landings were a big part of the reason. One side of the glider poked up from the rocks at a funny angle, and even from this distance, Ember could see torn fabric flapping in the breeze. But Gittel leapt up from amongst the wreckage, waving earnestly as she took a rope from her pack. She tied one end around a large rock and the other end around her waist, kicking off her boots as she dashed down toward the water. As she reached the water's edge, she leapt out into the current, swimming with strong, steady strokes toward Skye and Ember. As

she came close, she pushed herself upward, with Skye and Ember helping to pull her onto the rock.

"Are you OK?" she gasped, looking at her friends for any sign of injury.

Skye nodded and threw her arms around Gittel, and Ember joined in the hug.

"There was an avalanche," Ember tried to explain, "and ... oh Gittel! We have to get to the River Gate!"

Skye nodded earnestly, pointing out toward the canyon across the lake. "It's going to break. Ice and trees and a torrent of water. We have to warn them!"

Gittel nodded seriously. "Can you swim? Skye, you look exhausted!"

"We've got to," Ember said, though her arms and legs felt wobbly and shaky.

Gittel tugged on the rope, pulling it hard to make sure it was still secure. "Tie this around you," she said to Ember. "It will be easier to pull yourself across. I can help Skye. Come on." Tugging at Skye's backpack, Gittel soon had the binding strap free, loosening the broken clasp with her pocketknife.

"Thank you!" Skye said, laying the soggy pack down on the rock. "It almost took me under!"

"Ready?" Gittel asked with a smile. "Just lay back and kick your legs."

They slipped into the water, and soon they were making their way steadily toward the shore, Gittel with one arm holding her friend as Skye kicked with her legs.

Ember watched them for a moment, tying the rope around her waist and taking another nervous look toward the canyon. Then she plunged into the water, coming up in a spray of bubbles a short distance out from the rock. She wrapped a paw around the rope, and then another, pulling herself along through the water as she made her way toward the shore. As Gittel and Skye reached the shallow water, they rushed over to the other end of the rope, both of them pulling until finally Ember felt grass and stone beneath her. She struggled to her feet on wobbly legs and threw her arms around her friends.

"Thank you, Gittel!" she gasped. "I don't know how we would have made it without you."

Gittel grinned. "I made a mess of my landing. Flying is not my strong point."

"But you swim like a fish!" Skye said, looking thankfully at her friend.

Ember nodded, studying Gittel's damaged glider. Everyone knew Gittel didn't like flying. The heights made her stomach feel sick, and then there were her landings. And yet, she had done it.

"How did you get here so fast?" Ember asked in amazement. "Gittel! You must have flown like the wind!"

Gittel nodded. "Like a very terrified, wobbly wind!" she laughed. "As soon as I saw Skye in trouble, I knew I had to come. Finding another pilot would have taken too much time. Everyone is out searching in the mountains.

"Well, what should we do now?" Gittel asked. She glanced over at her glider and shook her head. "There will be more pilots on their way, once the other spotters get a message to Haven. But it could be quite a while."

Ember was already on her feet, untying the rope from around her waist and looking out toward the south.

"We'll have to go on foot," she said softly. "Are you able to run?"

Skye nodded with a shaky grin, but Gittel seemed a little worried as she laced up her boots. "Underground?" she asked nervously, though she knew it was the quickest way.

"Underground," Ember said with a serious nod. "Down through the Northern Cistern."

25

The Northern Cistern

The cisterns near Haven had been built a few centuries after the time of Hegel. The mountains near the village were full of natural caves and tunnels, and many large caverns had been discovered down by the Cascade River. It had taken many years to prepare them to store water. Walls were built, walkways constructed, and a system of pipes was run from the Backland Valley. It had taken ten years to build the river gates with waterwheels and enormous cogs that could close them to dam the river. This was the biggest building project in the history of Haven, bigger even than building the Lookout and the bastion at Glider Leap.

Though the river gates were only closed once every ten years, bears were always at work in the caverns, maintaining the waterwheels and cogs and pipes that pumped water up into the village. Every Cub had spent time down at the cisterns, listening to the chief builder Ruslan teach about pulleys and cogs and the power of water.

"Look at the teeth on this cogwheel!" he would say. "Beautiful! A work of art!" He used words like *torque* and *rotational frequency,* and when he talked about *pinions* and *axes of rotation,* there was a blissful look on his face that made all the Cubs giggle. "Oh, the smell of fresh grease on turning iron!" he would say, looking off into space as if he were reciting poetry. "There is not another smell like it! Isn't it wonderful?" He would look at the cubs seriously, then wink and grin. Ruslan knew there weren't many who loved building like he did.

Every Cub in Haven had to learn the basics of how the river gates worked, and they all had to memorize the maps of the twisting tunnels and caverns. *"A bear should know a little about a lot, before they learn a lot about a little."* It was a saying from way back before Hegel's time, and it was the way Cubs were taught from the time they were very small. You might be a baker one day, but first you should learn something about mountains and trees, of singing and flying and counting and words. And even of cogs and pipes and water cisterns, and the tunnels that joined them under the cliffs.

As the three friends clambered over the rocky ground, Ember was going over the directions in her mind. Two large boulders just ahead, and a shallow pond ... out past the three pines and then down toward the cliffs.

"There it is!" Gittel exclaimed, pointing toward a small opening just ahead.

It was the far exit to the Northern Cistern, rarely used except to check the river levels once every few weeks and to bring in lumber from the valley when it was needed. Ruslan had brought them all here once, a few years ago, pointing out the entrance before leading them back into the tunnels. There was a long passageway just past the entrance, and beyond that, storage rooms and walkways that led to the Cistern.

Ember glanced back at Skye, who waved with a tired smile, pausing for a moment to catch her breath.

"I'm doing better now," Skye panted. "That crash really knocked the wind out of me though. I think I'm going to ache tomorrow." Skye took off her flight cap for a moment, squeezing the last drops of water out of it before pulling it back down over her ears with a grin.

"Let's go," Gittel called, holding her lamp high with one paw as she stepped into the darkness. She turned back toward Ember and Sky for a moment, scraping her pack on the narrow entrance as she waved them on. "I can hear the water!" she called. "We have to hurry."

They took off into the darkness, feeling the cool, damp air close in around them as they made their way. Gittel jogged along in front, her pack jiggling in the dimness as Skye and Ember followed close behind. As they went further a strong wind began to whistle down the tunnel, cold and icy with the smell of fresh, mountain water.

"This way!" Gittel shouted, trying to be heard above the growing noise. She turned into a larger tunnel, racing along for a short way until she came to another turn. Ember remembered the directions as they went. Right again up here, and …

The noise was suddenly deafening all around them—the sound of wind and thundering, roaring water. "The Cistern!" Ember shouted.

They came through a small opening and out onto a narrow walkway, high above an enormous swirl of rushing water. A row of lamps dimly lit the walkway, stretching out into the distance to the other side of the cavern. As they raced out over the water, Ember felt the walkway sway, the wooden planks and slick ropes creaking with the weight.

"I hope they checked this recently!" Skye shouted with a worried smile. "I've had enough swimming for one day!"

Ember patted her on the back and nodded as encouragingly as she could manage. Her stomach was suddenly feeling queasy.

"Look at Gittel go!" Ember said, shaking her head in wonder. She was racing along the wobbling walkway and almost looked like she was having fun. Just then Gittel stopped and turned back toward Skye and Ember, her eyes sparkling in the lamplight and a wide grin spread across her face.

"I thought you didn't like the tunnels!" Ember gasped as they finally caught up.

"I don't," Gittel said with a smile, "but look at the water! Have you ever seen it so wild?"

Ember shook her head, and Skye chuckled. "You may not like flying," Skye laughed, "but when it comes to water, you're braver than a salmon."

Gittel's grin spread wider.

"And furrier!" Ember added. "Now, let's get off this bridge!"

Gittel turned and raced on along the walkway, turning from time to time to make sure Ember and Skye were keeping up.

As they came to the end, Ember leapt off onto the solid ground, thankful to be on the other side of the churning water.

"There are bears just ahead," Gittel shouted, pointing down another narrow tunnel toward moving shadows. As they came closer, Ember could hear shouts and calls and the sound of gears and creaking pulleys.

"Gittel?" shouted a voice, as they came out onto a long platform. "Ember? Skye?"

Ruslan was running toward them, his face looking puzzled and confused. Pepper was right behind him, her speckled fur smeared with dust and grease. She was Ruslan's daughter, still just a little Cub, but she had a love of building almost as strong as his.

"Come on!" Ember cried, racing past Ruslan and Pepper, out toward the river gates. "There's danger!"

Ruslan began moving at once, calling out to other bears as they hurried along the platform and out onto the gates.

Ember spun to a stop and peered northward, looking out over the water toward the canyon in the distance.

"There's danger," she gasped, as Ruslan came up beside her. "Avalanche ... up in the canyon. It took out a whole grove of pines. It could break at any time!"

Ruslan's face went pale. "Any time?" he asked gravely.

Ember nodded, and Skye stepped forward.

"It's big!" Skye said seriously, her eyes wide and earnest.

Suddenly Gittel let out a cry, pointing across the lake as a rush of water swirled out of the canyon in the distance. Enormous logs and splintered branches twirled like twigs amongst chunks of ice and muddy snow.

"Shut down the inlets!" Ruslan shouted, pointing to a couple of bears. "Get the gears switched. We have to get the gates ready to open!"

There was a rush of activity as bears ran off toward the platform and the cave that held the waterwheels and cogs. Everyone was shouting, pulling ropes and levers as the enormous cogs slowly began to move.

"The riverbed!" Ruslan gasped, turning to the three friends. "We can't open the gates till we know the riverbed is clear!"

The logs and ice still thundered out of the canyon, with a wall of water surging into the lake.

Skye was already moving, racing across the pathway toward the edge of the cave. "I'm going!" she shouted.

Pepper was right behind her, her little legs straining to keep up. "It's by the platform. See it there to the right?"

"The glider!" Ember exclaimed, nodding to Gittel and then taking off at a run.

A glider was kept in the cavern by the gates, used for carrying messages and supplies when they were needed quickly. Skye and Pepper already had it down when Ember reached them, and soon they were all tightening the poles and fastening Skye in the harness.

"I'll watch for your signal!" Ruslan said earnestly, glancing back at the splintered trees swirling out into the lake. "We don't have long, Skye. Fly as fast as you can."

Skye nodded, tugging on her harness straps one more time before looking up at Ember with a worried smile. "As fast as I can," she said, and then in a few steps she leapt out into the air and plummeted down toward the riverbed.

26
Riverbed Day

At first, there was no sign of Skye, then all of a sudden she burst out of the shadows, shooting toward the Backland Valley as her glider caught the wind. Ember watched her for a moment and then turned back to Ruslan, who was shouting directions to the bears on top of the River Gate.

"Hold the levers till I signal!" he was shouting, as he watched the wave of logs and ice moving quickly across the lake. He turned back toward the south, just in time to see Skye disappear around the bend that led out into the Backland Valley.

"Ten minutes!" he gasped, as Ember ran up with Pepper and Gittel. "She won't be able to warn them in less than that! It's going to hit us soon!" he said, nodding toward the wave. "We have to keep the gates shut! There will be little Cubs and their mothers out on the riverbed. We have to hold the gates until Skye can warn them."

Ruslan paused for a moment, his mind racing. "I've got to get up to the signal room," he said. It was a cave high in the cliffs on the north side of the river.

"I'll go!" Ember said eagerly. "You're needed here. Gittel and I can get there quickly. We know the way."

Ruslan seemed worried, but after a moment, he nodded. "If the gates break, you'll be stuck on the other side, but we'll send help when we can. Hurry!"

Ember and Gittel took off at a run, racing across the walkway that ran along the top of the gates. She could see the surging wave on the lake, a swirling froth of mud and ice tossing a jumble of logs and branches as it rose higher. Ember hurried up a short flight of stairs. Gittel was right behind her, gasping and panting as they ran with all their strength. There was a small landing strewn with coils of rope and stacked beams, and beyond that a doorway stamped with a picture of a fire.

Ember flung the door open, glancing back at Gittel for a moment before starting up another flight of stairs. "Three hundred and forty-eight." Ember could remember counting them as a little Cub. Three hundred forty-eight spiraling stairs, and then another big door that would open into the signal room. With a gasp, she pushed her body to go faster, circling higher and higher into the cliffs.

Skye looked down at the riverbed as it rushed by in a blur below. The cliffs of the Backland Valley rose high on either side of her, bathing the valley in deep shadows even in the middle of the day. The glider hummed and trembled as she rushed along, the sound of the wind whistling past her ears as she tightly gripped the steering bar.

"Come on!" she groaned, wishing the glider would go faster. Glancing to her left she could see the edge of Glider Leap, high up above her on the top of the cliffs. Soon she would reach the Cascade bend, the wide curve around Mount Hegel where the river turned south toward The Precipice. The little Cubs would be just a mile or so from there, down near the grassy place where most bears went for picnics. All the Cubs who were too young to be searching for Growly would be there with their mothers, looking for gems out on the dry Cascade riverbed.

"Come on!" she groaned again. She knew she was running out of time.

•◆•◆•◆•◆•◆•◆•◆•◆•◆•◆•◆•◆•◆•

Ember burst into the signal room, gasping and trying to catch her breath as she looked frantically around the room.

"Ember!" Gittel cried, pointing at one of the large windows that looked out over the river. The wave had already reached the edge of the lake and was swirling into the gorge toward the River Gates.

"Brace yourself!"

Ember heard Ruslan's shout of warning from somewhere below, echoed by other bears as they scrambled toward the cliffs. There was a sudden, thundering rumble, and then an enormous, shaking boom that sent Ember and Gittel tumbling to the floor.

Ember scrambled to her feet and raced over to the window, looking down to see a wash of spray shooting high into the air. It sent logs and chunks of ice swirling up over the Gates. Gittel's eyes were wide and her mouth gaped open. The air was filled with the noise of splintering logs and groaning metal.

"The signals!" Ember gasped. "Gittel! Start the signal fires. I'll loose the flags!"

Gittel nodded and raced to a large fire pit opening out onto the cliffs. It was filled with oil-soaked branches, and there were bags of powder to make smoke. She already had her flint out of her pocket, and in a moment, there were flames leaping up amongst the branches, and billows of thick red smoke swirled into the sky.

Ember tugged one of the long ropes on the wall, heaving with all her might as a row of flags unfurled high in the cliffs above the signal room. *Emergency ... Highest Danger!* It would be clear to the bears up on Glider Leap, and soon even the Lookout would see the smoke.

"Is it holding?" Ember cried, nodding toward the window where Gittel was standing.

Gittel glanced over at Ember, her face pale with fright. "I ... I think so!" she gasped. "It's hard to see with all the spray."

"Let's go!" Ember shouted, turning back toward the door and rushing off down the stairs.

The sound of shouts echoed up through the stairway as they raced downward, along with thumps and crashes and a terrible screeching that seemed to go on and on.

"There's the doorway!" Ember gasped, leaping down with a thump onto the landing and taking off again at a run.

Gittel gasped. Ahead of them on the platform was a scene of total chaos.

✦·✦·✦·✦·✦·✦·✦·✦·✦·✦·✦·✦·✦·✦·✦·

Skye swooped down over the rocks, scanning the riverbed ahead of her for any sign of movement. Just a little farther. There's the big apple tree with the rope swing on its branch, the grassy slope and the picnic shelter. There!

Skye pushed the nose of her glider downward, hurtling over the riverbed and crying out to the mothers and their little Cubs out amongst the rocks.

"Danger!" she cried, tilting her wings in the sign every bear of Haven knew. She swooped upward and turned hard, coming back around as mothers grabbed their little Cubs and began to scramble toward the riverbank. "Danger!" Skye cried again, watching to see if everyone had heard. Bears were calling out to each other now, running this way and that as they gathered all of the Cubs.

Skye breathed a sigh of relief, pulling back on the steering bar and sending her glider soaring higher into the air. She glanced back for a moment to see most of the bears were already on the riverbanks, and the others would soon be safely out of the path of the river. "Now to get above the mountain," she whispered, feeling the surge of a strong gust of wind.

⁘⁘⁘⁘⁘⁘⁘⁘⁘⁘⁘⁘

Ruslan stood out on the platform near the river, shouting orders as bears rushed toward the straining gears. "Hold the gates!!" he cried, looking desperately for any sign of Skye. Enormous logs and trees were strewn out across the bridge, and Ember could hear the mighty gates straining under the pressure.

"Everyone across," he shouted, "except for those at the levers. We need more bears on the other side!" There was a rush of movement from down below, and bears poured up onto the platform, racing toward the pathway that stretched out above the gates. "Come on!" Ruslan called, waving anxiously to Ember and Gittel.

They raced out of the cave and onto the bridge, leaping over logs and branches as they came into the sunlight. Ember could feel the gates trembling underneath her. Smoke poured into the sky above the signal room, and Ember could see the flags whipping wildly high up on the cliffs. "They must have seen it by now!" Ember thought to herself, stopping next to Ruslan for a moment as he gazed up into the sky above Mount Hegel.

"I can't see her!" he groaned. "I don't know if these gates can hold."

"Ice!" someone suddenly cried, pointing toward three enormous, jagged chunks tumbling and turning as they were swept into the gorge, heading straight toward them.

"Go!" Ruslan gasped, grabbing Ember by the paw and taking off at a run. The ice was rumbling toward the bridge, crunching against the cliff walls in a surge of water. There was an enormous boom as the ice slammed into the gates, sending Ember, Gittel, and Ruslan sprawling out onto the platform on the far side of the river. Bears were scrambling all around them, shouting in alarm as they raced to check the levers.

"There she is!" Gittel cried, pointing at a tiny speck zooming up above the peaks of Mount Hegel.

Ruslan already had his telescope in his paw. "She did it!" he gasped, and he spun toward the bears racing around him. "Open the gates!" he cried, taking off at a run toward the levers. "Signal the other side!"

Another bear shouted, taking a large yellow flag from a holder and waving it wildly. Bears down in the cave were already hauling on the levers, the enormous iron gears groaning. There was a sickening sound all around them, and a rumble from below as the waterwheels turned.

Ember felt the floor trembling under her feet, as dust and pebbles sprinkled down from above. And slowly, with a grinding boom, the gates began to move.

27
Gone

A thin spray of water burst through the gap in the gates as they slowly opened. It grew bigger and stronger until soon a mighty torrent roared. Logs and ice tumbled through the gap, digging up rocks and mud as a rush of water thundered down the dry riverbed toward the Backland Valley.

The gates were damaged. Ember could tell by the awful grinding that shook the cavern. As the minutes ticked by, Ember heard shouts and cries from the workers as they saw splintered beams and buckled metal. There were gliders in the air now. Ember could see them coming around the cliffs, circling high above the gates as they soared past the thick trail of red smoke from the emergency signal.

"Any sign of Skye?" Ember asked, turning to Gittel. She was scanning above the peaks with Ruslan's telescope.

Gittel shook her head. "She would have gone to Glider Leap, I think. To report what has happened."

Gittel took the telescope down from her eye for a moment and pointed at the gliders, which were circling back toward the Valley. "They'll be starting the search for Growly again, I imagine."

Growly! Ember felt a deep ache rising inside. In the chaos of the last few hours, she just had to keep moving. Now all the feelings were rushing back again, like the water surging through the damaged river gates.

"We've got to get back to Glider Leap," Ember whispered, her eyes suddenly stinging with salty tears.

Gittel looked over at her friend. "We'll have to go on foot," she said softly, coming near to give Ember a comforting hug. "If we run, we could be there by late afternoon. I'm up for it if you are."

Ember sniffled and wiped the tears away with her sleeve, looking at her friend gratefully for a moment before she nodded.

Ruslan was down on the floor of the cavern, inspecting the gates as they slowly drew back into the cliffs. Ember and Gittel heard his shouts as they came down off the platform; he had to speak loudly to be heard above the din.

"Three beams gone in that section! ... That brace will need to be replaced!" Pepper was standing next to him, busily scribbling notes in a book as he spoke. As Ember and Gittel came closer, he paused to give them a weary smile.

"They're looking rough," he shouted, "but did you see the beating they took?" There was tired satisfaction in his eyes. "Water levels higher than they've ever been ... and they still held!"

"We're going back to search for Growly," Gittel shouted. "We'll have to go on foot."

Ruslan nodded, putting his paw up to his chin.

"I wish we had more gliders. The other spare is still up at Glider Leap. It's a long walk back."

"We're going to run," Ember shouted shakily. She could feel the tears coming again.

Ruslan smiled at her kindly. "You better get going then. They need you back in Haven."

Gittel and Ember raced through the tunnels, scurrying up tall flights of stairs and on through the caves and caverns under the mountains. At times they came out into bright sunlight, their path taking them along narrow walkways on the face of the cliffs high above the Cascade River. They stopped occasionally, panting and gasping for breath for a few minutes before taking off again into the tunnels that led toward the Backlands. It was mid-afternoon when they reached a deep forest of pine in the valley. Soon the two friends came out into the sunlight at the place where the Cascade turns westward.

Ember could see Glider Leap, high in the distance, the shadow of a glider rippling down along the cliffs as it circled in for a landing. Gittel was stooped over and gasping as she tried to catch her breath.

"Are you OK?" Ember asked. They had been running for hours now, with only a couple of stops. Ember was soaked in sweat and she could feel her heart pounding in her chest.

Gittel looked up and grinned. "I'm ... I'm just getting warmed up!" she panted. "Ready?"

The two friends were off again, racing along the edge of the river for a while before turning up a twisting path that led toward the northern cliffs of Mount Hegel. Janika Mountain loomed out across the rough land, the jutting shape of Honey Guard outcrop bathed in late afternoon light.

"Almost there!" Gittel gasped. Her face was taut and pale. Ember was sure she must look the same. Neither of them had run like this before.

They jogged along the walkway, a strong mountain wind whipping past them as it whistled along the cliffs. They soon came to another narrow valley, scrambling down a rugged stairway and then up again on the other side.

"The Lookout!" Ember cried, pointing to the top of the tower peeking above the rocks. They were on the eastern end of the Little Cliffs, and just ahead would be one last tunnel that came out not far from the tower. The sun was low over the mountains now. Gliders were coming in from the east, swooping out around Janika Mountain on their way toward Glider Leap. Ember felt her heart sinking. No more flights would be going out. It was already too late in the day.

They came out of the tunnels into the crimson glow of sunset and the shouts of bears near the Lookout as they made their way down from the Leap.

"Ember!" one voice cried. "Gittel? How did you ... ?"

It was Edolie. She was with Calico and Ash.

As Ember saw Growly's mother, her eyes welled up with tears. Edolie looked exhausted, and her face was drawn with worry.

"He's gone, Ember," Edolie whispered, her voice croaky and hoarse. "There's no sign of him in the mountains. Not a single trace ..."

Ember threw her arms around Edolie, trying with all her strength to be brave. "Tomorrow we'll go out again. Oh Edolie ... he must be *somewhere!*"

Edolie nodded, wiping her eyes and taking a deep breath before she spoke. "Yes," she said ... her voice now sounding firm. "Tomorrow every glider will be out over the Lower Lands. We *will* find him, sweet Ember."

Ash looked over at Ember, not sure what to say. He and Growly were very close friends, and his heart was aching with worry. "Skye told us what you did," he said softly. "That was really brave. Growly would have ..."

Ember could see tears in the corners of his eyes. He looked down at his feet sadly, his voice trailing off as Gittel put her arm around his shoulder.

Just then, Skye came running down the path from Glider Leap, the fur on her cheeks already soaked with tears. "Ember!" she sobbed, flinging one arm around her friend and wincing a little. Her other arm was bundled in a makeshift sling.

"Oh, Skye! Are you all right?" Ember asked.

"It looks like a bad strain," Ash said seriously. "I wrapped it up as best I could. She's going to need to see the doctor once she gets home."

The little group made their way down the dusty street into Haven, breaking off quietly toward their homes to get some rest. They would meet at the Lookout an hour before dawn. Tomorrow all the bears of the village would be going out into the Lower Lands.

Ember turned the handle of the library door, pushing it open softly and coming into the bright light of the hall.

"Ember?" Merridy's worried call came from the main library room, and there was the sound of hurried footsteps before she burst into the entry hall. "Oh Ember!" Merridy threw her arms around her exhausted daughter and hugged her tightly. "I heard about the River Gate! Word came that you were OK. Oh Ember, I was so worried!"

"He's gone!" Ember croaked, tears welling up as she pressed her face against Merridy's cheek. "Mama ... he's gone!"

Merridy squeezed Ember tighter, fighting back tears of her own as she tried to speak. Her mind was searching for the right thing to say, but nothing seemed to come. "Oh Ember ..." she whispered, stroking the deep crimson brown fur of her daughter's cheek, her memories swirling back to a moment just like this, many years ago. Mika had comforted her in just the same way, here in the library.

"He's gone!" Merridy had sobbed it over and over, on the day C.J.'s glider went over The Precipice.

28
A Message in the Night

The library was quiet and still, bathed in warm, glowing moonlight coming through the windows. Ember tossed restlessly on her mattress, which was laid out next to Merridy's in the middle of the library floor. They often spent the night here, surrounded by the books and the light of the stars that glistened above the clouds stretching out beyond The Precipice.

"I don't want to be alone tonight, Mama," Ember had whispered, her red-rimmed eyes brimming with tears.

"Me either," Merridy had replied, holding her daughter tenderly. And they had stretched out their mattresses in the middle of the floor. Ember's gentle sobs had faded off into dreams.

In her dream, Ember stood amongst endless rows of books, looking down a long shelf that stretched back into the shadows. The shelf was filled with history books, and the stories of famous bears: of Heflin and of Benna, and the lands beyond the Great River. Of Janika, and the lost village, and Wynterlin, her friend. There were rows and rows of books on Hegel: biographies and novels, books of poetry, and songs.

In her dream, Ember walked slowly along the shelf, running her paw gently over the endless volumes and wondering why her heart ached in such a lonely way. As she went further back into the shadows, it seemed the wide library windows were suddenly very far away, and the soft pools of moonlight were just dim glimmers in the distance. She was standing at the end of the aisle, looking down at a thin little book that had almost slipped out of sight under the shelf. It was covered in dust, and as she picked it up, Ember had to wipe it with her sleeve to see what was written on the cover.

"*The Growly Book*," Ember gasped as she read the words, and her eyes suddenly welled with tears. "Growly!" she sobbed, her voice barely more than a croaky whisper.

With her paws shaking, she opened the little book.

"Growly, son of Farren and Edolie, grandson of Fergal and Mika. He went missing on his Adventure. He was a good bear ..."

"No!" Ember gasped, desperately turning empty pages as tears streamed down her face. "What about the time we built the tree house in in the hidden meadow? There should be at least a chapter on that! And the snowballs and skating, and the exploring with Ash and all the Cubs? What about that winter when we all got stuck at the cottage? There could be a whole book on that! And what about all the stories and poems Growly loved to write. They should be in here, too!"

Ember turned the empty pages in dismay, finally coming to the last one, which had just a little scribble, " ... a very good bear. The End."

Ember slapped the book closed, almost dropping it on the floor as she let out a sob. That couldn't be how the story went! Ember ran back along the shelf. There must be another Growly book somewhere!

"Tap, tap, tap." In her dream, it seemed like the whole library was suddenly filled with the sound of a clock or of a branch hitting against a window.

"Tap, tap, tap."

Ember looked down along the aisle, toward the large windows that were now right in front of her.

"Ember!"

Merridy's startled cry woke her suddenly from her dream. Ember sat up on her mattress, looking wildly as her heart pounded.

"Mama!" she gasped, as she saw Merridy's shocked face and her trembling paw pointing toward the library windows.

"Mama ... wha ... ?"

"Tap, tap, tap."

Ember looked over at the tall windows. The sky outside was filled with glistening stars stretching out toward the horizon and ...

Ember gasped. There on the ledge outside the window was a tiny shape, a dark silhouette against the starry sky. It was ... it was a bird!

"Tap, tap, tap."

Ember's eyes went wide as she suddenly realized. "C.J.'s signal! Mama! It's the bird!"

Merridy was already on her feet, stumbling across the floor on shaking legs. She turned to Ember, looking like she was about to say something, but no words would come out.

Ember leapt up from her mattress and raced across the floor as the little bird tapped again.

Now that they were closer, Ember could see the little bird looking in at them and nodding excitedly, his eyes sparkling happily. Even in the dimness, Ember could make out his bright blue and red coloring.

"Mama! Look!" Ember gasped. The little bird was tapping again, and nodding down toward a folded piece of paper that lay beside him on the ledge.

Merridy still couldn't speak. Tears were streaming down her cheeks, and it seemed as if her whole body was trembling.

"It's him, Mama!" Ember sobbed happily. She stumbled forward, and with a shaky paw pulled back the latch on one of the large windows. As she gently swung it open, the room was filled with cool mountain air. The little bird whistled happily, picking up the note in his beak, and then swooped down into the room, dropping the folded paper at Merridy's feet.

Merridy fell to her knees as she fumbled with the paper. "It's ... it's from ..." She looked over at Ember, her face pale with shock.

It looked to Ember as if Merridy might be about to faint. "Is it C.J., Mama?" Ember cried.

Merridy nodded. She was trying to say something, but it took her a few moments to even get a sound out. "And ... and Growly!

Ember blinked in shock, her mind racing to try and make sense of what she had just heard. Growly? ... Growly!

197

Ember felt like *she* was about to faint. "How?" The room was spinning and swirling and her heart was pounding in her ears as she looked up at Merridy through blurry tears. "Mama, *how?*"

"Look," Merridy whispered, handing her daughter the note.

Ember gazed down at the crumpled paper, staring at the scribbled words and trying to make sense of what she was reading. How could it be? It was Growly's handwriting all right. She could tell that right away. Countless times she had sat and read his poems and stories, scribbled in that same, wonderful way.

"*Merridy*," the message said, "*We are trapped on The Precipice. Our way is blocked by the Cascade Falls. Ask the mayor to close the river one more time, so we can come through. We have friends with us, and C.J. is alive!*"

And there was Growly's signature. There was no mistaking that!

At the bottom of the page was another message, written in a rough, trembly script that looked jagged and uneven. Ember recognized it right away, too. Even though it was jumbled she could see whom it was from.

"C.J.!" Ember whispered, looking up at her mother through eyes blurry with tears.

"*I'm coming home at last,*" it read. "*My love, I am coming home to you.*"

29

For Growly

Ember raced up the steep, mountain path. The sound of the breeze whistled past her ears and her heart pounded in time with the thud of her boots over the rocky ground. Gittel was right behind. Ember could hear the squeak of her friend's swinging lantern and the sound of her soft gasps.

"Don't slow down for me!" Gittel wheezed. Her face looked strained, but she was smiling and there was a sparkle of adventure in her eyes.

"We're almost at the stairs!" Ember gasped, suddenly realizing how far they had come. She had been so lost in her thoughts that the steep climb up the side of Mount Hegel had sped by almost without her noticing. Growly *and* C.J. were on The Precipice! The thought still made her head spin. She had gone to bed last night thinking Growly was lost and now ...

Ember's eyes welled with tears all over again. She let them flow freely down her cheeks. Ember was used to tears by now.

After reading the note back in the library, Ember had gazed up at Merridy for a long moment, her mind trying to make sense of what she had just read. Merridy had just stared back with her mouth wide, trembling and shaking as she took Ember's paws in hers.

"Oh, Ember!" she had whispered. And then she had said it again. This time it came out as a joyful cry, and the two of them had stood there in the middle of the library. They held each other tightly as tears streamed down their faces, and the room was filled with the sound of heavy, happy sobs and sniffles. It was just for a moment though. The little bird, who had been watching the two bears anxiously, let out a sudden chirp.

"Farren and Edolie! " Merridy gasped, stepping back from Ember and trying to think of what to do next.

Ember had looked up at her mother, sniffling back the tears. "I'll go, Mama," she gasped. Oh, she couldn't wait to tell Growly's parents the news!

Merridy nodded. "I ..." Merridy was trembling as she tried to get the words out, "I ... I've got to tell Fergal and Mika that C.J.'s ... " She couldn't finish the sentence. Her eyes were still wide in astonishment, as if she were hearing the news of C.J. and Growly all over again. Merridy blinked, and then all of a sudden she raced off toward the hall as the little bird flapped up into the air, and with a joyful whistle sped off after her.

Ember ran after her mother and the bird as they burst out the front door and into the street. "Mama!" Ember cried, grabbing her coat from the peg in the hall as she rushed by and pushing one arm through the sleeve as she tried to keep up. "Mama!"

Ember had stumbled out into the street just in time to see Merridy disappearing down the road into the night. "Mama! You're still in your pajamas!"

There had been a moment of silence and then a howl of laughter burst through the darkness. "Yes! Yes, I am. And C.J. is COMING HOME!"

Merridy's happy shouts echoed through the village, filling the early morning stillness with joyful sound. Lights soon appeared in windows and bewildered bears stumbled out into the street. By the time Ember had reached Growly's home, Haven was already filled shouts and cries of joy as the news began to spread.

Once they got past the shock, Growly's parents wasted no time—Farren calling out orders and Edolie organizing the girl Cubs to send messages and bring supplies. Ropes and medical kits were gathered, lanterns were lit, and rescue packs collected. Ember's friend, Calico, was sent to ring the town hall bell, and Laila had gone to her parents' store to help pack food.

Most of the bears of the Rescue Committee were already down in the Lower Lands. They had slept the night there in the Westwind Caverns, ready to continue the search for Growly at first light. Ash was assigned to take them the news.

Skye was sent to light the signal fire. Her arm was bundled up in a fresh sling, but she had assured Farren she could still run, even if it did hurt her shoulder a little bit. "The doctor says I won't be flying for a while, but even with one shoulder I can run like the wind! Oh, please let me help." And so she had raced off into the darkness, heading toward the Lookout and the signal fire up on the hilltop beyond.

And Ember ... From the moment she had read Growly's note, she knew what she had to do. Someone had to take a message to Ruslan and the bears at the River Gate. They had to try to get them closed one more time. They had to stop the Cascade River so Growly and C.J. could have a chance of getting home.

"I can do it," Ember had said earnestly, looking up at Farren and taking a deep breath. "They're on The Precipice. We have to hurry."

Farren had been silent for a long moment, his face tight with concern. Everyone knew the dangers of a night flight.

It was Edolie who spoke first, resting her paw gently on her husband's shoulder. "Look how she has grown, Farren," she said quietly. There was a sound of wonder in Edolie's voice.

Farren was quiet a little longer, and then suddenly he nodded. "Go, Ember!" he said.

There had been a quick farewell to Merridy. The librarian's face went pale with worry at the mention of the night flight. But it was only for a moment. There was a confidence in Merridy's eyes, and when she spoke her voice was strong and sure. "You can do it, brave Ember," she said with a smile. "My dear sweet Cub, you're not a Cub anymore!"

⋅•⋅•⋅•⋅•⋅•⋅⋅•⋅•⋅•⋅•⋅•⋅

Gittel and Ember had raced past the Lookout, kicking up dust and sending loose rocks tumbling down the slopes as they made their way toward Glider Leap. Gittel carried a small backpack, filled with Ember's flight clothes she had brought from the library.

Now, as they came up the final stairs and through the doorway into Glider Leap, Gittel opened up the pack and handed the clothes to Ember. "Flight pants," she said, tossing them to Ember, "and your jacket ..." A grin spread across Gittel's face, " ... and ... this." Gittel stood slowly to her feet, holding up a long, beautiful dress for Ember to see. It was streaked with deep purples and reds and a flicker of fiery gold.

Ember looked at it in quiet surprise, a smile spreading across her face. "My favorite!" she said softly.

Gittel's grin spread wider as she nodded, "And Growly's, too! He said it looks like a sunrise. He said you looked very ... ummmm ... *nice* ... in it. I thought you might want it when you see him."

Ember threw her arms around Gittel, giving her friend a trembling hug.

"Thank you! Oh, Gittel. My stomach is in such knots. I don't know if I can even get up onto the platform!"

"That's what I'm here for," Gittel laughed. "I'll carry you and your glider all the way to the Hidden Valley if I have to! Come on!"

Gittel heaved Merridy's glider out of its storage rack. "I'll need to adjust the bindings of this one," Gittel laughed, "since you decided to take yours for a swim!"

<hr/>

There was a strong breeze up on the platform, fresh with the smell of ice as it blew in from the mountains. There was a hint of fall in that smell and a chill that sent a shiver down Ember's back. Out over the Backland Valley, all was shadow—the dark shapes of the cliffs rising above the river.

"Look!" Gittel cried, standing up from the outstretched glider, which tilted and wobbled in the wind. Far down on the hills above the Lookout, a twisting blaze of flame was twirling up into the air.

For Growly

"It's Skye!" Ember shouted with a smile. "She's started the signal fire."

The flames rose higher into the sky, glowing brightly on the top of the hill.

Ember turned her gaze over the Backland Valley. "Come on!" she whispered, peering off into the distance.

Moments passed, and then more. Still nothing.

Gittel had the glider lifted, and she waved anxiously for Ember to get harnessed.

"It's so hard to see!" Ember said in a quivery voice. Her legs felt as if they wouldn't hold her up, and she began to sway as she tried to hold the glider in place.

"For Growly and C.J.," Gittel whispered, helping Ember steady the glider.

"For Growly and C.J.," Ember nodded, and with a sudden push, she ran out across the platform. Her boots thudded heavily as she moved faster and faster. She could faintly see the edge of the platform coming closer as she picked up speed. Ember's heart pounded, but the wobbliness in her legs was gone. "And for Mama!" she whispered, and she leapt out into the darkness.

30
Night Flight

Ember felt herself twisting and falling through a world of night and shadows. She swooped down into the Backland Valley, plummeting past the cliffs until a strong updraft lifted her soaring above the Cascade River. She could make out the dim, white crests of the rapids and the faint glimmer of moonlight on the spray far below. Glancing back, Ember could see the glow of Gittel's lamp, falling farther and farther behind her as she raced over the valley. She was near the cliffs. Ember could see them rising, dark and towering into the sky, blocking out the light of the stars. Cliffs and shadows ... in the darkness it was hard to tell which was which!

Ember swerved up to the right and felt her heart leap as she plunged into a thick patch of deep shadow. She was starting to panic. Ember could feel her heart racing and her paws shook wildly as she tried to hold on to the steering bar. The wind was icy and it roared past her ears, making her feel like the cliffs and shadows were starting to crumble and fall.

All of a sudden, one of Ember's trembling paws slipped from the bar, and the glider lurched sharply to the left, sending her speeding through the darkness toward the cliffs. She let out a panicked cry, looking around wildly to try and see anything in the darkness. Suddenly the cliff wall appeared, looming through the shadows right in front of her. Ember pulled on the steering bar with all her might, soaring upward as she tried to turn back toward the right. Her eyes were wide with fear. It was so hard to see where to fly in this darkness.

Suddenly a shadow sped by right in front of her, and the air was filled with the sound of a shrieking cry.

"Goldentail!" Ember gasped. She had heard that cry many times flying out amongst the mountains. Ember still couldn't see much ahead of her. She had come too close to the cliffs and the deep shadows of the mountains. But Goldentail's cry cut through the darkness. In a moment, the enormous bird swooped back around and rushed past the glider just a short way ahead of her. As they came out of the shadows, Ember caught a glimpse of the eagle's white and golden tail feathers, and beyond, far up in the distance, a sudden flash of fire.

"The signal!" Ember breathed a sigh of relief, tightening her paws on the steering bar as the glider soared back out over the valley. There was Janika

Mountain! Ember recognized the dark outline rising up against the stars. And there was the opening to the river gorge, with the blazing signal fire now bright up in the cliffs.

Ember swung the glider down into the gorge, swooping between the narrow cliffs as Goldentail let out another cry. The Cascade River roared, echoing off the cliff walls as it thundered through the mountains.

Ember let out a happy shout. Her heart still thumped wildly, but the panicked feeling was slipping away, as if it were being blown by the whistling mountain wind. There was the tunnel through the cliffs and the winding walkway. She recognized it all now. And there were the mighty river gates, pulled back into the caves, with the signal fire blazing high above them in the cliffs.

Goldentail let out a joyful call, and with a sudden turn, flew back toward his home.

Ember pulled back on the handle, lifting the nose of the glider and then swinging it downward to the right. She had done this hundreds of times. Every pilot Cub had to learn to land on the platform at the River Gate. It was a tricky landing, with a tight turn and a sudden drop, but Ember knew the turns by heart. In a moment, her feet touched the platform and she pulled the glider to a running, thudding stop.

"Ember!" A cry came from the stairs next to the landing platform. It was Ruslan, still in his grimy work clothes, his tired face smeared with grease and soot. His daughter, Pepper, was just ahead of him, racing up onto the platform to help with the glider.

"Ember?" Pepper gasped. "It's still night!"

Ruslan tugged on the glider straps, helping Ember loose herself from the safety harness. He was exhausted, and Ember could see even little Pepper looked like she had been working all through the night.

"We saw the signal fire a short while ago," Ruslan said. His voice sounded worried. "All the bears here are awake and ready, but we weren't expecting a glider till daybreak."

"A night flight!" Pepper gasped, looking up at Ember in wonder.

There were shouts now in the cavern, and other bears were coming up on the platform.

Ember pulled off her flight cap and dropped her pack to the ground. "Oh, Ruslan!" Ember cried. "We have to close the river gates!" She pulled Farren's note out of her pocket and handed it to the tired bear as she continued. "Growly is on The Precipice! And C.J. is with him! We have to stop the river so they can make it back home!"

Pepper let out a cry, and Ruslan blinked in shock. "C.J.?"

There were gasps amongst the nearby bears, and Ruslan took in a long, deep breath. "Close the river gates?" he gasped. "I don't know if ... " His voice trailed off as he lifted Farren's note in his shaky paw and read.

A hush had fallen over the gathered bears, with just the faint sound of whispers as more bears arrived. Ruslan stared down at the note, his mouth moving slightly as he read the words.

"C.J.!" he whispered, folding up the note and looking up at Ember as a tear trickled down his cheek. "I knew him when I was just a little Cub ... I thought I would never see him ... " Ruslan's voice trailed off and he was silent, lost for a moment in memories. The tired look began to slip away, and he suddenly addressed the gathered bears. "Prepare the cog wheels!" he said loudly. His voice was strong.

Pepper looked up at her father in surprise, and there were a few gasps from other bears.

"I know the gates are damaged," Ruslan said firmly, "but Growly is trapped on The Precipice. And he has C.J. with him! We have to try to get the river gates closed again!"

There were cries of astonishment and shouts as the news spread.

"To your stations!" Ruslan shouted, his voice rising above the din. "Signal the bears across the gorge! Sound the bell!"

There was a sudden rush of activity. Shouts and clanging filled the cavern, and bears raced in all directions, hauling ropes and chains and slamming cogs and levers into place.

Ember stood on the platform, watching. There were more shouts and bangs and signal flashes from the bears on the other side of the gorge.

Ruslan ran back and forth on the platform, calling out orders and glancing nervously at the thundering river. The gates were still badly damaged, even after all the bears' work through the night. It would take weeks to get them back to their full strength again. But if Growly and C.J. had a chance of being rescued ...

Long minutes ticked by, and then more and more, until finally Ruslan lifted a bright yellow and green striped flag, and there was a sharp blast as the alarm horn was sounded.

"The levers!" Ruslan shouted, his voice lost amongst all the noise. The bears knew what to do though. Suddenly the whole cavern shook, and with a groaning shudder, the battered river gates began to move.

31
The Plummet

The river surged against the enormous gates, swirling and frothing as it rose higher and higher. "Open the overflow cistern!" Ruslan cried to Pepper. Ever since the river gates had been set in motion, she had been running messages and gathering signal flags, then returning to her father's side, ready to move as soon as he called.

"The green and red flags!" Ruslan shouted, smiling fondly as his daughter sped back up the stairs with them already in her paws. Pepper knew all of the flag signals. Even the ones that were rarely used.

Ember watched from the platform, trying to not get in the way of the other bears as they raced to do their tasks. The gates were closed now, but the river was rising quickly. Most of the cisterns had been filled yesterday, and there were not many places left for the water to be held.

"Third cistern full!" Pepper cried, pulling on her father's arm. There was a bear on the other side of the gorge, desperately waving an orange flag with a large green circle in the middle.

"It's too fast!" Ruslan groaned. "Quick Pepper ... wave the flags now! We have to get the overflow cistern open *now!*"

Pepper raced out to the edge of the river gates, waving her flag in wide, high swoops in the bright lantern light there. A moment later, a green flag went up on the other side. Green was to say that the message had been seen.

"We haven't got long, Ember," Ruslan said gravely. The alarm in his voice sent a chill down Ember's back. "We have maybe an hour till the overflow is full, but ... " Ruslan could hardly stand to say the words out loud, "but I think we might lose the gates before then!"

Ember could hear the creaking of the damaged beams and the screech of buckling metal, and under her feet she felt a tremor that made her stomach quiver with fear.

There was a sudden, deep boom from somewhere far below, and then another screeching noise echoed through the cavern.

"Pepper! Fetch the red flag!" Ruslan shouted in alarm. "The red flag with the black stripe." He looked back at Ember, his face drawn and pale. "They're starting to break!" he gasped. "Ember, we don't have very long!"

Ember felt panic welling up inside of her. How long had the gates been closed? Fifteen minutes? Half an hour? In all the commotion she had lost track of the time. What if it wasn't enough for Growly and C.J. to make it? What if the little bird hadn't been able to return Merridy's message in time?

"Run, Growly!" Ember whispered.

"You must go now!" Ruslan said firmly, shaking Ember out of her thoughts. "Warn any bears that are close to the riverbed. Warn them now, Ember! Go!"

Pepper appeared from the stairs and came back onto the platform, the bundled red flag in her paws and tears streaming down her cheeks. Everyone knew what the red flag meant: Abandon all stations. Abandon the gates.

"Help Ember," Ruslan said kindly, doing his best not to sound alarmed. "She needs you, Pepper, to help her get ready to fly."

Pepper nodded as bravely as she could, handing the bundled flag to her father and looking up at Ember with a sniffle. "I'll get the harness ready," she whispered.

Ruslan raced out across the platform, loosening the flag as he ran. Coming to the edge of the River Gate, he lifted the flag high into the air, waving it in sweeping arcs, his feet planted wide and firm on the trembling ground.

Ember pulled on her flight cap, tightening the strap and adjusting her goggles. She had bundled her dress earlier, rolling it up under her coat to make it easier to fly. She quickly checked that it was still tied tightly. It wouldn't do to have her dress loose and flapping in the middle of a flight.

"It's ready!" Pepper shouted to Ember proudly as she lifted the harness for Ember to see.

Ember hurried over to the glider, fastening straps and hoisting the steering bar as Pepper did a final check.

"All set!" Pepper said shakily. There were still tears in the corners of her eyes.

Ember could see that the Cub was doing all she could to sound brave. "Thank you!" Ember said, giving Pepper a soft smile. Then pointing toward Ruslan who was still waving the red flag out along the platform, she added, "Your daddy will need you now."

The sound of alarm horns continued to fill the air, and the toll of a signal bell rose up above the grinding rumble and the shouts.

"Run, Growly," Ember breathed again, and then she was off along the platform and leaping out into the dark.

As she swooped down over the riverbed, Ember could make out the dim shapes of twisted logs and boulders scattered along the gorge. It was still very dark, but the light of the signal fires glistened softly on the dripping cliff walls where the river had been. Ember heaved back on the steering bar, lifting the nose of the glider and sending it soaring upward on the strong breeze as she came whooshing out of the gorge.

The Cascade Lift is what they called this wind. It was always here in the Backland Valley, a steady updraft that came in around the mountains. Ember soared into the dark sky, racing past the rocky cliffs as the wind took her higher. She could see the fire on the mountains near the Lookout, twisting and crackling brightly—sending trails of twirling sparks high into the air.

And far across the valley, Ember could see the top of Glider Leap, glowing brightly with lamplight high up between the peaks of Mount Hegel.

Ember pushed the glider higher, soaring upward in a curving turn until she was far above the cliffs. And now ... the Plummet. Ember pushed the nose of her glider forward and lunged downward in a steep dive. The

Plummet was the fastest glider route from the Backland Valley to the Lower Lands. A breathtaking swoop around the Lookout above the roofs of Haven and then a plunge over the Little Cliffs and out over the forests far, far below.

Ember pushed the nose of her glider lower, speeding down over the slopes and past the signal fire toward the Lookout.

The streets of Haven were blazing with light, and as Ember whooshed overhead she could see bears running to and fro with bundles and ropes as they made their way toward the Little Cliffs. Most of the bears were already in the Lower Lands, many still in their pajamas as they made their way toward The Precipice. Ember could see tiny flickers of lamplight far out over the Lower Lands, some already way down near the bridge used to cross the Cascade River. Merridy would be one of them—Ember was sure of it.

The Little Cliffs were just ahead. Ember pushed her glider even lower, swooping down over the last of the rooftops as her glider picked up speed. "And now the plunge," Ember whispered to herself, " ... three, two, one ... and ... "

The ground dropped away beneath her as she reached the edge of the cliffs. Ember tilted the nose of the glider hard, sending her into a steep, whistling dive down the side of the mountain. "Seven ... six ... five ..."

Ember counted down the seconds in her mind, " ... and ... PULL!"

Ember heaved back on the steering bar and the glider whooshed out into the sky, swooping high over the forests and into the Lower Lands. Far in the distance she could see the long line of The Precipice, with the first rays of morning light beginning to show above the clouds.

"Run, Growly!" Ember whispered. "Oh, *please,* run with all your might!"

32
Return

Ember raced over the Lower Lands, the wings of her glider humming in the whistling wind. Treetops rushed past in a blur below her, then wide-open meadows and gently sloping hills, all dim and nestled in darkness. The sunrise was coming. Ember could see the first light of it beyond The Precipice, a soft, orange glow down amongst the blanket of clouds that stretched as far as could be seen beyond the cliffs.

Just ahead, Ember could see a long, twinkling line of little lights, moving steadily down the road that led over the Cascade River and on toward the cottage in the hidden meadow. Lamplight. Hundreds of lamps carried by the bears of Haven as they ran to search for Growly and C.J. There were more lights coming down the stairs on the Little Cliffs. Ember could also see small glimmers moving down from the village.

She was following the path now, racing silently above the curving trail until she reached the long line of bears. There were shouts of surprise as she swooped down over the crowd, and then cheers as they recognized the glider.

"It's Ember!" came a shout from somewhere down below, and the message raced along the line as Ember whooshed by overhead.

They were almost at the river. Ember could see the curving line of the riverbed, silent and empty now that the river gates were closed. And there was the bridge. The line of lanterns stretched out across it. Ember felt her heart thump with alarm. She could see bobbing flickers of lantern light down out in the riverbed.

"The bridge!" Ember cried, shouting with all her might. "To the bridge! Danger!"

Turning her glider hard to the right, Ember swung back in a tight curve, looking desperately for the best place to land. The river gates could break at any time. They might have already broken, and the thunderous torrent of the Cascade could be coming at any moment.

Seeing an open stretch, Ember came to a running stop in the soft, cool grass. Bears ran to meet her, with lanterns swinging wildly and their shouts getting louder as they hurried down from the road.

Ember fumbled with the straps of her harness, loosening the bindings, then stepping back from the glider as the first of the bears came near.

"Mama!" Ember cried, seeing the familiar face of Merridy in the glow of the lanterns. "The riverbed! We have to get everyone out of the riverbed! The gates were still holding when I left Ruslan in the mountains. But he's certain they can't hold for long. When the water comes, it will come quickly. We must get everyone out of the riverbed."

There was a crowd of bears around Ember now, and as they heard her message, shouts of warning were called and some rushed back to help clear the riverbed.

"Get everyone across the bridge quickly!" Farren shouted. He had reached Ember just after Merridy. "Adwin, will you stay and watch at the bridge?"

Gittel's father nodded and began to move back toward the river.

"Everyone," Farren continued, raising his voice for all to hear. "We don't have long! Run with all your strength to the hidden meadow."

In a moment they were off, racing along the dusty path that led into the hills. Minutes passed, and they seemed like hours to Ember. She kept waiting to hear the roar of the river somewhere back behind her, but as the time stretched on, the only sound was the grunts and gasps of the bears as they ran, and the pounding of their boots as they came into the narrows. The path cut into the hills, with tall walls of jumbled stone on either side, twisting past a stream and then between two jagged cliffs.

Just up ahead was a small patch of trees, and just beyond that ...

"The meadow!" Ember gasped.

The darkness of the night was slipping away. Through the trees Ember could see a glow of deep red and orange and purple. As they came out onto the open grassy slopes, Ember could make out the rough boards of the cottage and the patterns of carvings on the window frames and doors.

The bears hurried up a gentle slope, spreading out through the long grass as they came into the meadow.

"Start down at the riverbank!" Farren was shouting, calling out directions as the bears came into the meadow. "There may be a place down by the river ... " His voice trailed off into silence as the ground began to shake.

"The river!" Ember shrieked, panic welling up as the rumble turned into a roar.

"Look!" Merridy cried in dismay. She was pointing toward The Precipice. Against the bright light of the sunrise, Ember thought she could see the tiny shadow of something moving ... of some *things* moving, far in the distance, down in the bottom of the riverbed.

Farren was already running, with Edolie right at his side as the roar grew louder and louder all around them. Ember couldn't move for a moment, frozen by the sight of the tiny figures as they scrambled between the boulders. There was more than one ... Ember was sure of that now ... but it seemed like ... like there were even more than two.

"Run!" came a voice.

It was Merridy. Ember looked up at her mother, but Merridy's eyes were fixed on the movement in the riverbed.

Just then there was a sudden, booming crash, rising up above the roar as an enormous wall of water thundered out of the mountains and down along the riverbed.

"Run!" Merridy cried again, and now she was moving, racing after Edolie and Farren as the Cascade surged down toward The Precipice. Jagged chunks of splintered log and twisted metal beams were caught up in the surge, hurled along the riverbed by the roaring wall of water.

"The gates!" Ember gasped, her voice lost in the noise as she raced along after Merridy, trying to catch up. Everything felt slow, like a moment stretching on and on in a dream. The thud of her boots on the grass felt strange and far away, and the spray of the water seemed to glisten on the sunlight as it burst into the air. There was the little bird, flying off past Farren, flapping frantically as he raced toward the tiny figures far down in the riverbed at the edge of The Precipice.

Ember could see a shape up on the riverbank, stretching down and pulling ...

The water swept past on her left, roaring down the riverbed at a frightening speed. It would reach The

Precipice in moments. The figures were still scrambling, trying to get up the steep riverbank. They were never going to make it.

There was a sudden crash of water as the river smashed into a large boulder, sending a shower of spray high into the air.

Merridy let out a cry of dismay as the view of the riverbank was lost and the swirling waters of the Cascade burst out over The Precipice. "C.J!!!" she wailed, tumbling to her knees as Ember dropped down by her side.

Ember's eyes were bleary with tears as she tried to see through the glistening spray. Bright beams of sunlight pierced up over The Precipice, as the deep colors of the sunrise stretched out into the meadow.

"Look, Mama!" she cried.

There, far down by the riverbank, a tiny figure was climbing to its feet, and another, and another.

"Four!" Merridy gasped, her eyes suddenly wide in astonishment.

Ember leapt to her feet, looking over joyfully at Farren and Edolie. Growly's parents had stopped too, terrified Growly had been lost in the torrent.

"They made it!" Ember cried. "Look! LOOK! They made it!"

They all stood there for a moment, hardly able to move.

Four tiny figures were standing down beside the river. Ember blinked and rubbed her eyes. Four!

"Come on!" Merridy shouted. She was up and running again, waving frantically to the other bears as she bounded through the grass.

Edolie and Farren were running too, calling out happily to Mika and Fergal who were not far behind. "Growly!" they were shouting. "C.J. and Growly!"

Ember leaped down through the meadow until she reached Merridy's side. The figures were coming closer. Ember could see them clearly now, two taller ones, one holding up the other, and two smaller ones beside them.

The sunrise filled the meadow with warm light and sent long shadows dancing out in front of the figures.

As they came closer, Merridy raced out ahead, faster than a bear her age should ever be able to run. Her dress swirled out behind her, catching the light as it fluttered in the wind.

Ember felt herself slowing, and as she looked over at Farren and Edolie, she noticed they were slowing down, too. It seemed all the bears had come to a stop, watching as Merridy came near the little group.

It *was* Growly. Ember could recognize his face now, caked in mud, his clothes worn and tattered. He had his arm around an older bear. That must be C.J. And beside them, two strange little creatures, also caked in dust and mud—both with wide, joyous grins spread across their faces.

As Merridy got closer she stumbled to a walk, standing on wobbling legs for a moment in front of Growly and the older bear. Ember could see her mother was trembling, her shoulders shaking softly with her sobs. And then her arms flung around the older bear's neck. All was silent. Ember hardly dared to breathe. It seemed as if even time itself had paused to make sure it didn't interrupt this wondrous moment. And then, as if some secret signal had been given, the gathered bears let out a booming, joyous cheer and ran to surround the little huddled group.

Ember didn't move yet though. She had been watching the wonderful meeting, lost in an overwhelming joy, and then her eyes had drifted to Growly, and ... and he was looking right back at her. His fur was matted and caked with dirt, and his face was smeared with mud and grime. But his eyes ... his eyes were bright and clear and ... and he was looking right at her.

Ember felt her legs trembling, and she was sure her face was turning bright red. She looked down for a moment, and it was then that she noticed her beautiful dress was still bundled up around her waist, tied above her flight pants to make it easier when she was flying.

"My dress!" she gasped, but when she looked back up at Growly she could see it didn't matter. He was home! Growly was home! Ember raced down toward the joyous group, and as she absentmindedly tugged the string and set her dress flapping gloriously around her, she didn't even notice.

33

What Lies across the River

A twirling flicker of white danced past Ember's nose, swirling up into the sky for a moment before twisting down across the platform of Glider Leap.

"Snow?" came a happy shout. It was only partly a question. Mostly it was a cry of utter joy. Chippy jumped up from where he was sitting, chasing the twirling snowflake as it was lifted on the mountain wind. "SNOW!" he cried, leaping in the air and sending the little flake twirling out toward the edge of the platform.

"Chippington!" Annily gasped, looking over at Ember and shaking her head.

Ember grinned. She and Annily had become close friends in the weeks since Growly and C.J. had returned. Annily was a monkey. That was what they called these wonderful creatures. They were smart and funny and ... had never seen snow.

Annily leapt up and joined Chippy as he chased the drifting flake, finally catching it on her paw, to the laughter and cheers of everyone.

Skye was there, in her flight cap and coat of course. And Gittel, too. They had all come up to Glider Leap this morning, early before the sunrise on this special, special day. Ash was standing not far from Chippy, looking at him with a happy grin. Ash loved the monkeys. Well ... *everyone* loved the monkeys. Haven had been abuzz with the news of Growly's journey and the astonishing places out beyond The Precipice. There had been meetings and storytellings and question upon question. And as soon as C.J. had regained his strength, there had been meetings and questions all over again. Chippy and Annily had become the talk of the village. Everyone wanted to have them over for dinner or lunch or breakfast. There were morning teas and afternoon teas and invitation after invitation, until finally the mayor had to ask the village to give these new friends a little time to rest.

Annily was staying at the library with Ember, and they had talked long into the nights about everything you could imagine, and more than just a little about Annily's friend, Chippy.

"We're getting married, someday," Annily had said with a sigh. "If ... *when* we find a way home."

Annily spoke Bear as well as most bears. Growly had said that of all the monkeys she was one of the best at it.

Chippy was quite good, too. He had a wonderful accent that made all the bears grin. Little Cubs would gather around him and plead for him to say something in Bear. *Anything!*

Chippy didn't mind. He would talk to them for hours and chase the little Cubs as they squealed happily down the main street of Haven.

It had taken C.J. almost two weeks to fully recover. The doctor had looked very anxious at first, coming out of his room with a worried sigh and a hug for Merridy.

"He is very weak. We've never known of a bear taking so much Aventhistle. But he is strong, Merridy. I think we can get him well again."

And he had gotten stronger, until finally he was up and walking through Haven with a look of pure delight.

"I wondered if I would ever see it again," he might say. Or, "I'd almost forgotten how colorful the doors are."

And Merridy was always by his side, holding his paw tightly and beaming with joy.

C.J. had officially proposed on the day he returned, sending the worried doctor out of the room to speak to Merridy privately. They had talked for over an hour before C.J. slipped into unconsciousness.

Merridy had come out of the room, cheeks streaked with tears and eyes red-rimmed from crying. At first Ember had thought it was because C.J. was so sick, but Merridy had shaken her head silently as more tears came.

"No, no, sweet Ember," she had whispered, when words could finally come. "He has asked me to be his wife. Oh, it was beautiful! I could have never imagined hearing it would sound so wonderful!" Merridy was quiet for a moment before she continued. "But he's worried ... that there might be a chance you may not want to be his daughter."

"Oh Mama!" Ember's face burst into a grin, as tears welled at the corner of her eyes. "Of course I ... why would? Oh, Mama. OF COURSE! Oh, how I've longed for him to make it home."

Merridy was grinning, too, looking joyfully at Ember through the sniffles.

"I told him we would need time to think about it," she said with a wink. "No sense rushing into these kind of decisions."

"OH, MAMA!" Ember laughed. "*Please* tell me what you *really* said!"

Merridy smiled fondly at her daughter. "Yes!" she whispered. "I just said, yes ... *yes* ... YES!"

Over the weeks, Ember, Merridy, and C.J. had spent a lot of time together, sipping tea in the library and visiting all the places he had longed to see through the years he was gone. He was staying with Fergal and Mika while he recovered, but after breakfast he was always ready to visit old friends and see all that had changed over the years.

Ember loved to hear his stories and see the joyful smile that was now always on her mother's face.

"I think we make a wonderful family!" Ember sighed one afternoon, snuggling between Merridy and C.J. as they sat telling stories on the couch.

"We are quite good looking!" C.J. laughed, giving Merridy a wink, but when he looked over at Ember there was a tear of thankfulness in his eyes. "At least the two of *you* are! I need a bit of a trim."

And then there was Growly. Ember looked over at him now, bundled warmly in his new coat and a thick scarf, his brown fur tousled by the wind and his eyes sparkling happily as he watched Chippy and Annily studying the snowflake. How wonderful it was to have him home again. It felt like years he had been gone ... not just the summer. They had spent hours together talking, and Ember had listened with eyes wide as he told about the places beyond The Precipice.

"Were you scared?" she had asked, and he had grinned shyly and nodded.

"Almost all the time. Except when I was eating!"

That had made Ember giggle, and Growly had looked at her with a wonderful, loving smile. "I ... I thought of you over and over," he stammered, "every single day."

Growly had stayed close to C.J. in the weeks the older bear was recovering, sometimes sleeping on the floor at the foot of C.J.'s bed, to be there in case he woke up and needed help in the night. And Chippy would be there, too, curled up in a chair through the late hours. Growly and Chippy. There were already legends beginning to swirl about them.

"We just wanted to find C.J.," Growly kept insisting, "and to find a way back home."

Growly had listened in amazement when he heard of all that had happened while he was gone. "A night flight!" he had gasped, looking at Ember in astonishment. "Ember ... how ... ?"

His look of admiration made Ember blush. But she had to admit it was wonderful to see him look at her that way. It was that moment she knew that one day they would be married. One day, when the time was fully right. She had always thought they might, but this time she knew. "You're a bear worth waiting for, Growly," Ember had thought with a smile. And now, watching him up on Glider Leap, it went through her mind again.

"The first snow, Chippy!" he was saying. "Though we can't really say 'first snow' till a Cub catches one on his tongue in the main street of Haven. It's a big event, you know. I'm thinking it might happen sometime in the next few weeks."

Growly seemed different now. More than just a few months older. Perhaps it was all the places he had been, all the things he had been through, but to Ember he seemed ... almost grown up.

Growly suddenly jumped up, sticking out his tongue as another snowflake swirled into view. "Dun leh meee faw ov the mow-tain," he mumbled, trying to talk while he chased the snowflake with his tongue.

Ember giggled and shook her head fondly. "*Almost grown up!*" she thought with a smile.

The sun was starting to rise in the east. Here on Glider Leap you could see it long before it appeared down in the village. Ember took one more look around as she picked up her pack and got ready to leave. Haven was beginning to wake up. Everyone would be getting up early today.

Skye was staring thoughtfully toward the Great River, into the misty clouds that hung far out over the water. They had all spent time up here over the last weeks, looking out through the telescope for any sign of fire, or anything on the other side of the Great River.

"There must be *something* over there," Growly had said, when Ember had told him about the fire she had seen, "and Skye saw it, too. She's got eyes like an eagle."

But there had been no sign of anything except the swirling cloud and spray and brief glimpses of green out in the distance.

Today wasn't the day to be searching though. Today would be the biggest celebration any bear in Haven could remember.

Growly looked over at Ember and grinned. "migh ... beee ... layy for ... va ... weh-din ... " he said with a chuckle, still with his tongue out as he tried to catch the snowflake.

Ember laughed—a big, loud, joyful laugh that drifted on the air like a dancing snowflake. These were her friends, and this was her home, and her mama was getting married!

34
Family

All the bears of Haven were there, stretching out in long rows on the grassy slopes near the cottage. This is where Merridy and C.J. had wanted to be married—in the peaceful, hidden meadow at the top of The Precipice.

Ember stood on the soft grass in front of the cottage, wearing a brand new dress with a string of daisies around her neck and a beautiful bunch of wildflowers held tightly in her paw.

Growly was there, standing over with his parents, looking a little uncomfortable in a suit coat and fresh ironed pants. He had his favorite old boots on though. Merridy had told him that he *must* wear those boots. They had taken him all the way to C.J. (and back again). Growly looked down at them now and then grinned over at Ember. She was wearing her favorite boots, too.

Chippy and Annily were standing next to Growly. The two monkeys looked small amongst the bears, but Ember hardly noticed anymore. They had become so loved by the bears of Haven that it almost seemed as if they had always been around. Annily gave Ember a wistful smile that made Ember giggle. They'd talked a lot about weddings over the last few weeks.

Skye had a new dress and flowers in her flight cap. And Gittel was in a new dress, too, back near the long tables loaded with refreshments.

"There will be more cakes than Haven has ever seen!" Gittel had promised, when Merridy asked her to help with the food. Looking at the groaning tables now, Ember was pretty sure Gittel was right.

And there was C.J., standing just across from Ember, with Tully, the little red and blue bird, perched on his shoulder. C.J. looked over at Ember and gave her a loving wink before he turned back toward the cottage. His eyes had been fixed on the front door for the last half an hour.

"The signal!" Ash shouted, pointing up to a Cub, who waved a flag on a nearby hill.

The mayor, who had been standing next to Fergal and Mika, suddenly stepped forward and lifted his paw for quiet.

"It is not the usual tradition," he said, "but in light of all that has happened, these are not *traditional* days. A bear we thought forever gone has suddenly come back here to his home. A bear has come back from The Precipice, and that has *never* happened. When I asked C.J. and Merridy what song they would most like to hear at their wedding, do you think it was 'With My Love Through the Sparkling Twilight?' No! The song that they wanted was the silliest of the silly Adventure songs, 'Adventure My Bear, Adventure!' That's what they wanted to hear! This is just *NOT* tradition!" The mayor looked out at the gathered bears, pretending to look upset for a moment. Everyone could see the twinkle in his eye though. Suddenly a smile spread across his face, and he let out a happy laugh. "I LOVE it! What better song for such an astonishing couple?"

There was a loud cheer, and then everyone burst into song, singing with all the might and joy and fun that such a day demanded. In the midst of the song, the little cottage door opened and Merridy stepped out into the sunlight, her face beaming and bright, with happy tears streaming down her cheeks. She was dazzling, more than any elegant dress or bouquet could have ever hoped to make her.

Ember gasped. "Oh Mama," she whispered. "Mama, you are *beautiful*."

High above, a line of five gliders swooped in from the mountains, showering the gathered bears with flower petals that fluttered down like gentle snow.

Ember looked up and sighed, reveling in the joyous moment as the petals rained down around her.

"Home," Ember whispered. "This is my home."

<hr />

The trail of bears moved slowly across the Lower Lands, singing and laughing as they made their way back toward Haven. There had been long farewells and well-wishes to C.J and Merridy, and Gittel's mother had probably asked at least seven times if the married couple had enough food. "Perhaps just a *few* more cupcakes?"

They would stay there in the cottage for a few weeks, just the two of them. Ember smiled as she walked along the path. She had seen the pantry ... they would definitely *not* get hungry.

The smell of fall was in the air, and the trees were beginning to blaze with bright orange and red and yellow. And then would come the snow, and the long, frosty winter with open fires and hot tea and ... family. Ember felt her heart leap and the smile on her face spread wider. *My* family.

She could see the buildings of Haven now, nestled high up on the cliffs, with the Lookout rising above the rooftops. It was a good place ... a *wonderful* place. A place where an orphaned baby Cub could find family and home. Ember looked up at Growly, who was a little way ahead, and smiled as she thought to herself, "And a place where that bear could one day start a family of her own."

The sun was beginning to set now. Long shadows stretched down from the mountains, reaching out over the forests and meadows. The bears on the trail were taking out their lanterns, and soon there was a blinking, glowing line stretching out across the Lower Lands as they made their way back to Haven. As the trail of lights went on toward the village, Ember let out a happy laugh and moved up next to Growly, the sound of an old Adventure song rising up into the night.

the end

Join the Growly Club for FREE
and get exclusive access to:

behind the story videos

early book release offers

downloads, printables, & newsletters

and more Growly fun!

www.thegrowlyclub.com

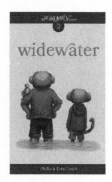

About the Authors

Philip and Erin Ulrich live in South Carolina with their two daughters. They enjoy adventures in the wild, as long as they can be home in time for dinner. Being Australian, Phil probably has natural-born abilities to hunt and wrestle dangerous creatures. He has used these natural abilities to finish in the top four in family balloon volleyball. An avid reader at heart, Erin loves to sit with a warm cup of coffee on a comfy chair and wishes these amenities were easier to find in the wild. Together, they run their own business, Design by Insight (designbyinsight. net), a website and book design company.

Phil and Erin are currently at work on the continuing adventures of Growly.

About the Illustrator

Annie Barnett is a creative soul who spends her days making art, memories, and inevitably a good mess – whether it's with curry, paint, or play dough. She now plays house in the Hudson Valley, where she lives with her husband, three lovely daughters and an occasional pet ladybug. Her artwork can be seen at BeSmallStudios.com.

Acknowledgements

To our two sweet girls—thank you for going on this adventure with us. We love you!

To those who have walked with us throughout the Here We Go journey—thank you for believing in us and encouraging us along the way.

To Annie Barnett—you took our words and captured them perfectly in your illustrations. Thank you so much for your untiring passion for excellence and amazing talent.

To Sandra Peoples—thank you for your sharp eye and wisdom in editing our manuscript. We have learned so much from working with you!

Made in the USA
Middletown, DE
06 March 2021